Erle Stanley Gardner and The Murder Room

>>> This title is part of The Murder Room, our series dedicated to making available out-of-print or hard-to-find titles by classic crime writers.

Crime fiction has always held up a mirror to society. The Victorians were fascinated by sensational murder and the emerging science of detection; now we are obsessed with the forensic detail of violent death. And no other genre has so captivated and enthralled readers.

Vast troves of classic crime writing have for a long time been unavailable to all but the most dedicated frequenters of second-hand bookshops. The advent of digital publishing means that we are now able to bring you the backlists of a huge range of titles by classic and contemporary crime writers, some of which have been out of print for decades.

From the genteel amateur private eyes of the Golden Age and the femmes fatales of pulp fiction, to the morally ambiguous hard-boiled detectives of mid twentieth-century America and their descendants who walk our twenty-first century streets, The Murder Room has it all. **>>>**

The Murder Room
Where Criminal Minds Meet

themurderroom.com

T0352443

Erle Stanley Gardner (1889–1970)

Born in Malden, Massachusetts, Erle Stanley Gardner left school in 1909 and attended Valparaiso University School of Law in Indiana for just one month before he was suspended for focusing more on his hobby of boxing that his academic studies. Soon after, he settled in California, where he taught himself the law and passed the state bar exam in 1911. The practise of law never held much interest for him, however, apart from as it pertained to trial strategy, and in his spare time he began to write for the pulp magazines that gave Dashiell Hammett and Raymond Chandler their start. Not long after the publication of his first novel, *The Case of the Velvet Claws*, featuring Perry Mason, he gave up his legal practice to write full time. He had one daughter, Grace, with his first wife, Natalie, from whom he later separated. In 1968 Gardner married his long-term secretary, Agnes Jean Bethell, whom he professed to be the real 'Della Street', Perry Mason's sole (although unacknowledged) love interest. He was one of the most successful authors of all time and at the time of his death, in Temecula, California in 1970, is said to have had 135 million copies of his books in print in America alone.

By Erle Stanley Gardner
(titles below include only those
published in the Murder Room)

Perry Mason series

The Case of the Sulky Girl
(1933)
The Case of the Baited Hook
(1940)
The Case of the Borrowed
Brunette (1946)
The Case of the Lonely Heiress
(1948)
The Case of the Negligent
Nymph (1950)
The Case of the Moth-Eaten
Mink (1952)
The Case of the Glamorous
Ghost (1955)
The Case of the Terrified
Typist (1956)
The Case of the Gilded Lily
(1956)
The Case of the Lucky Loser
(1957)
The Case of the Long-Legged
Models (1958)
The Case of the Deadly Toy
(1959)
The Case of the Singing Skirt
(1959)

The Case of the Duplicate
Daughter (1960)
The Case of the Blonde
Bonanza (1962)

Cool and Lam series

The Bigger They Come (1939)
Turn on the Heat (1940)
Gold Comes in Bricks (1940)
Spill the Jackpot (1941)
Double or Quits (1941)
Owls Don't Blink (1942)
Bats Fly at Dusk (1942)
Cats Prowl at Night (1943)
Crows Can't Count (1946)
Fools Die on Friday (1947)
Bedrooms Have Windows
(1949)
Some Women Won't Wait (1953)
Beware the Curves (1956)
You Can Die Laughing (1957)
Some Slips Don't Show (1957)
The Count of Nine (1958)
Pass the Gravy (1959)
Kept Women Can't Quit (1960)
Bachelors Get Lonely (1961)
Shills Can't Count Chips (1961)

Try Anything Once (1962)
Fish or Cut Bait (1963)
Up For Grabs (1964)
Cut Thin to Win (1965)
Widows Wear Weeds (1966)
Traps Need Fresh Bait (1967)

Doug Selby D.A. series

The D.A. Calls it Murder (1937)
The D.A. Holds a Candle (1938)
The D.A. Draws a Circle (1939)
The D.A. Goes to Trial (1940)
The D.A. Cooks a Goose (1942)
The D.A. Calls a Turn (1944)
The D.A. Takes a Chance (1946)
The D.A. Breaks an Egg (1949)

Terry Clane series

Murder Up My Sleeve (1937)
The Case of the Backward
  Mule (1946)

Gramp Wiggins series

The Case of the Turning Tide
  (1941)
The Case of the Smoking
  Chimney (1943)

Two Clues (two novellas) (1947)

Beware the Curves

Erle Stanley Gardner

An Orion book

Copyright © The Erle Stanley Gardner Trust 1956

The right of Erle Stanley Gardner to be identified as the author of this work has
been asserted in accordance with the Copyright, Designs and Patents Act 1988.

This edition published by
The Orion Publishing Group Ltd
Orion House
5 Upper St Martin's Lane
London WC2H 9EA

An Hachette UK company
A CIP catalogue record for this book is available from the British Library

ISBN 978 1 4719 0900 9

www.orionbooks.co.uk

FOREWORD

FOR some years now my Perry Mason books have included Forewords describing interesting characters in the field of legal medicine. The books have been dedicated to the people described in the Forewords.

In the books I am now writing about Bertha Cool and Donald Lam (under the pen name of A. A. Fair) I want to depart from the field of legal medicine and tell you readers something about interesting personalities in the administration of justice.

That field includes law enforcement, crime investigation, and penology.

Few people realize the extent to which penitentiaries are in effect crime factories. Professional penologists know some of the reforms which are needed but they hesitate to speak out because of public apathy in some instances, and public hostility in others.

My friend Arthur Bernard is the Warden of the Nevada State Penitentiary at Carson City.

This is a small prison, so small that Art Bernard knows all of the inmates personally.

Bernard started his career in penology some years ago as a political appointee. He became interested in his work and interested in trying to find out the causes of crime.

It is a peculiar thing that very few criminals know why they took up a life of crime in the first place. Like everyone else they are inclined to rationalize and quite frequently to blame others.

Some of the inmates of the Carson City penitentiary won't even give a warden the time of day. Others are vicious, depraved killers. Some of them are shrewd "cons," who will cheerfully tell any investigator anything he wants to hear which they think will result in some benefit, however slight, to themselves.

There are, however, a large number of prison inmates who want to complete their sentences and then go straight. Whether they can do so or not is another qestion. Some of them will, many of them won't. Society imposes terrific handicaps upon a man who has just been released from prison.

Art Bernard is doing a lot of work with these prison inmates, trying to help them, trying to find out how it happened they became law violators.

Art Bernard has a tape recorder in his office and, when one of these men gets to a point where he is willing to talk and talk frankly, Art Bernard interviews him, puts the interview on tape, listens back to the tape recording, makes his own comments and suggestions, then sends the tape recording to Dr. LeMoyne Snyder, the medico-legal investigator, and to me. I make duplicates of these tape recordings and we are gradually building up quite a library. Slowly but surely we are getting significant clues to *some* of the underlying impulses, drives, urges, and weaknesses which cause men to run afoul of the law.

It is an interesting work and I feel that it is a valuable work.

Art Bernard has been a miner; a prize fighter, a cattle and sheep rancher and broncobuster, and a state inspector of mines. He knows human nature, and to a very large extent he is self-educated.

Because he is essentially modest, he tends to minimize the very wonderful education he has given himself in the school of hard knocks. But because he has always dealt in the realm of practice rather than theory, and because so much of his knowledge was acquired at first hand in the hard way, he is essentially and entirely practical. He has little use for theory as such. He won't touch anything unless he feels sure it will work, and his background and training have been such that when he starts doing anything he makes it work.

Art Bernard tells me that some of the greatest tragedies of prison life come from the fact that the first offender has a minimum sentence of one year to serve.

Altogether too many of these first offenders are young men in the formative years of their lives. They are men who might well have been your sons or my sons. They have been guilty of some infraction of law and because of that have been sentenced to prison. They may have graduated from a field of juvenile delinquency and many of them have chips on their shoulders. However, in virtually every instance they have no real concept of prison life.

Perhaps the typical young man who is sent to prison for the first time acts as something of a smart aleck. He tries to swagger his way through life and he tries to be tough. That is largely a pose which he has adopted to reassure himself.

When the prison doors first clang shut on such a young man, when he first realizes the horror and degradation of prison life, when he is plunged into an existence of men deprived of women but not of sex, when he encounters the restrictions imposed by armed guards, strict discipline and narrow cells, there is a feeling of revulsion and of horror.

Art Bernard contends, and many thoughtful penologists agree, that if it were possible to release these young men from prison after they have been there just long enough to get a strong taste of prison life and to realize what it really is, they would never commit another crime as long as they lived.

Unfortunately, the minimum sentence is for a year. The young human male is remarkably adaptable and, as Art Bernard expresses it, after the first few weeks when the horror wears off the young man "becomes acclimated to prison life."

After that there are two strikes against him, or perhaps it would be better to say, two strikes against the society which sent him to prison in the first place and which maintains the institution in such a manner that it is a veritable crime factory.

There is great need for reform in our prison institutions, particularly in regard to the first offender, as well as to the weak-willed individual who has drifted into a life of crime following the paths of least resistance.

There is no space available here to comment on these matters, but I do want to call attention to the work that my friend Art Bernard is doing in making an intelligent study of people about whom society should have a lot more information.

So I dedicate this book to my friend, ARTHUR E. BERNARD, Warden of the Nevada State Penitentiary at Carson City, Nevada.

ERLE STANLEY GARDNER

CHAPTER ONE

BIG Bertha Cool displayed all of the ingratiating mannerisms of a hippopotamus acting coy during the season of courtship.

"Donald," she cooed, "I want you to meet Mr. Ansel, Mr. John Dittmar Ansel. This is Donald Lam, my partner, Mr. Ansel."

John Dittmar Ansel, a tall drink of water with the dark eyes of a poet, a thin straight nose, sensitive mouth, a profusion of wavy black hair, long tapering hands, and quiet clothes, was sitting very straight in his chair. He got up to acknowledge the introduction. His eyes were seven or eight inches above mine. I placed him at around six feet two or three. His voice was well modulated and quiet. His handclasp was the somewhat timid grip of a man who shrinks from physical violence.

It was difficult to imagine any greater contrast than that existing between big Bertha Cool and John Dittmar Ansel.

Bertha, seated behind her desk, went on in her most ingratiating manner, the diamonds on her fingers scintillating in the light from the window as she gestured with her hands.

"John Dittmar Ansel," she explained, "is a writer, Donald. Perhaps you've read some of his stuff—I mean his material."

She paused, anxiously.

I nodded.

Bertha beamed.

Ansel said apologetically, "I don't do a great deal of fiction, mostly technical articles. I use the pen name Dittmar."

"He has a problem," Bertha went on. "Someone recommended us to him. He asked for me because the name on the door 'B. Cool' made him think I was a man."

Bertha smiled at Ansel and said, "He was very gentlemanly about it, and was most considerate in making excuses, but I recognized the symptoms. I told him my partner was a man and I wanted him to meet you.

"If we can serve Mr. Ansel, Donald, we will, and if we can't there's no hard feelings, no hard feelings at all."

Bertha's lips were smiling affably. It was more difficult for her to control the expression in her avaricious little eyes that were as glittering cold as the diamonds on her fingers.

Ansel looked dubiously from Bertha to me, from me to Bertha.

Bertha, a hundred and sixty-five pounds of woman, somewhere in the late fifties or early sixties, as tough, hard and rugged as a coil of barbed wire, now smiling and purring in a manner so exaggerated that it was obviously phony, evidently

1

didn't appeal to Ansel. Ansel was still standing. He quietly manœuvred his position across the office so that he was between Bertha and the door.

He looked at me, hesitated, and apparently was trying to find some way of saying what was on his mind without hurting my feelings.

Bertha hurried along with a line of sales patter, talking fast, trying to get her ideas over before Ansel got out of the door.

"My partner Donald Lam is young, and he doesn't have the build you'd expect of a private detective. But he has brains, lots of brains, and because he looks so . . . so——"

Bertha, obviously groping for a word, suddenly decided the game wasn't worth the effort of being polite and nasty nice. Tossing her cooing manners to one side, she quit talking in her tone of assumed culture, and got down to brass tacks.

"Hell," she snapped, "he looks so goddam innocuous he can move around in the background and get all the dope he wants without anybody having any idea he's a private detective. He's a brainy little bastard, and you can gamble on that.

"Now then, do you want us or not? If you don't, say so, and get the hell out of that door because we're busy. If you do, come back here and sit down and start talking turkey. You give me the jumps standing on one foot and the other, like a guy waiting in front of the door at a boarding-house bathroom."

That did it. Ansel's sensitive mouth twisted into a smile. He came back and sat down.

"I think I want you," he said.

"All right," Bertha told him, "it's going to cost you money."

"How much money?"

"Tell us your problem and we'll tell you how much."

Ansel said, "Writers are not exactly over-burdened with money, Mrs. Cool."

That line got him no place.

"Neither are detectives," Bertha snapped.

Ansel's eyes lowered to look at her diamonds.

"Except the good ones," Bertha hastily amended. "What's on your mind?"

"I want you to find someone."

"Who?"

"I've forgotten his last name. His first name is Karl."

"You kidding?" Bertha asked.

"No."

Bertha looked at me.

"Why do you want to find him?" I asked.

Ansel ran long fingers through his dark, wavy hair. He looked at me and smiled. "He gave me an idea for a whale of a story," he said.

"When?" I asked.

"Six years ago."

"Where?"

"In Paris."

"Why do you want to find him?"

"To see if I can get the exclusive right to use the story."

"Fiction or fact?"

"Fact, but I want to turn it into fiction. It would make a powerful novel."

"All right," I said, "you met Karl in Paris. Lots of Karls go to Paris. What else do we have to go on?"

"I knew his last name at the time, of course, but I find that it's slipped my mind. He came from around this part of the country, a place by the name of Citrus Grove which is a suburb of Santa Ana. He was rather wealthy and he was on his honeymoon. His wife's name was Elizabeth. He called her Betty. She was a nice girl."

"What was the story about?" I asked.

"Well, it was about a marriage situation . . . I—It was about a man who convinced the girl he loved but who didn't love him that her real sweetheart was——" He stopped.

"I don't want to give away the plot of a perfectly good story," he said.

"All right," I said. "We're supposed to find a man by the name of Karl from Citrus Grove who went to Paris six years ago on his honeymoon, and who has the plot of a good story that you can't tell us about.

"What did he look like?"

"Tall, hard, broad-shouldered, a driving personality, the sort who gets what he wants."

"How old?"

"About my age."

"How old is that?"

"I'm thirty-two now."

"How did he make his money?"

"I don't know."

"What did he do for a living?"

"Investments, I think."

"How rich was he?"

"I don't know. He seemed to be fairly well fixed."

"That's rather a general term."

"It's the best I can do."

"Blond or brunette?"

"Redheaded."

"Eyes?"

"Blue."

"Height?"

"Six feet."

"Weight?"

3

"Heavy. Around two hundred and fifteen or twenty. Not fat. Sort of thick, if you know what I mean."

"Troubled with weight?"

"I suppose so, but he didn't diet. He ate what he wanted. He got what he wanted."

"You don't know what hotel he stayed at?"

"No."

"Don't know whether he went over by air or boat?"

"I think it was by boat, but I'm not sure."

"What month?"

"July, I think. I'm not certain."

"What do you want us to do?"

"Just locate him. Get me his name. That's all."

"All right," I said "We'll do it."

"How much will it cost?"

"Fifty dollars," I told him.

Bertha's desk chair gave an indignant squeak as she abruptly leaned forward. She opened her mouth, started to say something, then changed her mind.

I could see her eyes begin to flash. She was blinking the eyelids rapidly and a slow flush crept up on her face.

"Where can we reach you?" I asked Ansel.

"How long will it take?" he wanted to know.

"Probably not over a day."

"You can't reach me," he said. "I'll be in at this same time tomorrow afternoon." He gave me his hand, a light sensitive grip of long fingers.

He bowed to Bertha Cool and dissolved out of the door.

Bertha could hardly wait until the door had clicked shut. "Well, of all the namby-pamby, diffident, weak-kneed bastards!" she said.

"Him?" I asked.

"You!" she yelled.

"Why?" I wanted to know.

"No retainer!" Bertha screamed at me. "Nothing down even for expenses! No address! A lousy fee of fifty dollars for finding a guy by the name of Karl who was in Paris six years ago. And you're going to find him for a flat fifty bucks and not a damn cent down. You let that guy ease out of the office without so much as a red cent by way of retainer to cover expenses. You fix a flat fee of fifty bucks for doing something that may cost us a thousand."

I said, "Calm down, Bertha. The guy is a writer. Someone gave him an idea for a plot in Paris six years ago. He doesn't make much money. It was a factual story the man gave him, but he's going to turn it into fiction and make a novel out of it. So he wants to find the guy, and quite naturally he employs a detective agency to locate this bird. It's just routine."

4

Bertha shook her head as the full implications of what I was saying dawned on her.

"Fry me for an oyster!" she exclaimed.

"Exactly," I told her.

"I never thought of it that way now," Bertha said.

"Start thinking of it that way now," I told her.

"Well, what the hell does he *really* want?" she asked.

"Perhaps we can find out by tomorrow afternoon. It *could* be that he's writing an article on detective agencies, exposing the manner in which they try to stick their customers exorbitant fees for simple jobs.

"You know the way some of those newspapers do. They send a person with a perfect radio around to the different radio repair shops and see how many of the shops hook the guy for new tubes, elaborate repairs, and things of that sort."

"Pickle me for a goddam beet!" Bertha said.

I walked out.

CHAPTER TWO

THE newspaper office opened at eight-thirty. I was there at eight-thirty-five. I said I wanted to see the back files of six years ago.

No one even asked me who I was. I was given the back files all nicely bound together.

On the assumption that a honeymoon in Paris in July of six years ago probably meant a June wedding, I concentrated on the June issues, and by eight-forty-seven was looking at a picture of Karl Carver Endicott, flanked by a picture of Elizabeth Flanders. The bride had been employed as a secretary in a local law office. Karl Carver Endicott was the town big shot, orange groves, oil wells—"popular young businessman ... far-flung oil empire."

I made my notes, handed the papers back to the girl at the desk. The girl thanked me and smiled. She put her toe on a concealed buzzer button. I could see her weight shift. She wanted to be damn certain the alarm sounded.

I heard the buzzer in the inner office. A door opened and a young chap with long hair and sharp eyes came out of the inner office. He pretended to be looking for something then his eyes came to focus on me. "Oh, hello," he said, "anything I can do for you?"

"Thanks, I'm all taken care of."

"Nothing I can help you with?"

"Nothing."

It was okay by me. It just showed they were on the job. A man shows up from outside of town, wants to go through the files of the paper of six years ago. It might be nothing. It might be a story. If it was a story, naturally they wanted it. They didn't want a competitive paper to get it. If it was nothing, they didn't want to waste time.

I decided to let them know it was nothing.

The girl behind the counter said, "He was just looking over some of the back files."

The reporter said, "Oh yes," and looked at me inquiringly.

I laughed. "Doing a little research work on increase in property values. Attractive land was advertised as being for sale six years ago, and I wanted to find the price it sold for."

"Did you?" he asked.

I shook my head. "Just found that the property was for sale. I've got to hunt up the realtor now and try to find out what I can about price. It may not be too easy."

"It may not," the young man agreed. "Of course it would depend somewhat upon whether it was business property or ranching property."

6

"It would, wouldn't it?" I said.

He grinned.

I could have walked out at that time and nothing would have happened, but I had been lulled into a sense of security. I had had things so easy I wanted to get it all buttoned up.

"By the way," I said, "there's a chap by the name of Endicott here who has some acreage for sale I understand."

"Endicott?" he said.

"Karl Carver Endicott," I told him.

The reporter tried to swallow the expression of startled surprise on his face and didn't make a good job of it. The girl back of the counter dropped a dating stamp she was holding in her hand, and didn't stoop to pick it up. The reporter gulped a couple of times and said, "Did you know Endicott?"

"Shucks, no!" I said, "I'm interested in property, not people."

"I see."

"I could be looking for a lease," I told him.

"You could," he said.

Well, I'd gone that far. I might as well go the rest of the way. "All right," I said. "What's wrong with Endicott?"

"It depends on how you look at it."

"He still lives here, doesn't he?"

"He's a short distance outside of the city." The blue eyes were watching me as a cat watches a rat hole.

"There's just a chance," I said, "I may know the guy at that. I met an Endicott who came from this part of the country several years ago. He was abroad on his honeymoon."

"I see," the reporter said.

"Look," I said, "is anything wrong with Karl Endicott? Has he got the plague, or something?"

"Karl Endicott," he said, "was murdered a short time after he returned from his honeymoon. In case you're interested there's a reward of twenty-five thousand dollars for information leading to the arrest and conviction of the person or persons responsible for his death. And if you're snooping around on a live lead we'd sure appreciate getting the story."

"Murdered?"

"Murdered."

"Who offered the reward?"

"The Board of Directors of his company, Endicott Enterprises."

"Well," I said, "it's nice having met you."

"You haven't *met* me yet."

I grinned, "No, I didn't get your name, but of course I know who you are," and then added, "and I guess murder cases don't have anything to do with scouting out pieces of property."

I walked out of the door.

I'd driven down to Citrus Grove in the agency heap and had parked the damn thing almost in front of the door. I didn't dare get into the car so I walked over to a real estate office. I went in and chatted generalities with the realtor for a few minutes about this and that and these and those. I went out and had breakfast. I walked over to the public library, found it didn't open until ten o'clock, went to another real estate office, went to a phone booth and thumbed through the telephone directory.

The reporter was still following me.

I saw an officer going around checking the parking time on automobiles. The last thing I could afford was to have the car tagged, so I went to a restaurant, had a cup of coffee, went towards the back where there was a sign "Rest Rooms," closed the door behind me and walked out to the kitchen.

The cook, scooping up fried eggs from a hot plate, motioned with his thumb and said, "Over that way, buddy."

I just grinned at him, walked through the kitchen and out into an alley.

I walked down the alley, detoured a block, then cut across to my car as fast as I could without running.

The officer was just putting a tag on the car and the reporter was standing beside him with his notebook. I said to the officer, "I'm sorry, officer. I was just coming to get in the car."

"You're a little late."

"I didn't think your ordinance started until 9 a.m.".

He pointed to a diamond-shaped sign at the corner. "Parking one hour, 8.30 a.m. to 6 p.m." he said. "Sundays and holidays excepted."

I gave him my best smile and said, "You should make some concessions for out-of-town people."

"You own this car?"

"I drive it."

"Let's take a look at your licence," he said.

I showed it to him.

"Okay," he said. "I'll let it go this time."

The reporter grinned like a Cheshire cat.

I got in the car and drove away, leaving behind me a nice little story. I could even see the headlines in my mind's eye. "LOS ANGELES DETECTIVE INVESTIGATES LOCAL MURDER."

They could go on from there. "*Donald Lam, Junior Partner of the firm of Cool & Lam, Private Investigators of Los Angeles, was in town this morning, consulting newspaper back files, checking on the murder of Karl Carver Endicott.*

"*Lam refused to be interviewed, refused to give his name to a reporter, and quite plainly was interested in getting information rather than giving it. Nevertheless, the fact that this private detective agency is investigating ... etc., etc., etc.*"

8

All right. So what? Damn it, if our client had put his cards on the table, I wouldn't have led with my chin.

The fact remained I was mad.

I thought of how Bertha had described me as a brainy little bastard. I thought of how our phony client with the poetic features, the dreamy eyes and the long, sensitive fingers, was going to look at me when someone sent him a clipping from the Citrus Grove paper.

To hell with him! I'd have the thing all finished before the paper came out. He'd wanted information. I'd give it to him.

I drove back to the city and telephoned Elsie Brand, my private secretary.

"Hi, Elsie. Bertha in?"

"Yes."

"Restless?"

"Somewhat."

"Belligerent?"

"No."

"Did you see a client we had yesterday, a man by the name of Ansel?"

"No."

"He called yesterday afternoon about three o'clock. He's to be back at the same time today. Now get this. At exactly a quarter to three I'll be over at the bar across the street. The bartender knows me. Give me a ring there the minute this fellow comes in. Don't tell Bertha that you've been in touch with me or that you know anything at all about me. Okay?"

"Okay."

I hung up and went to the public library.

There is a master index published, giving the names of all authors who have appeared during each year in any of the major periodicals published in the United States.

Thirty minutes after I arrived at the library I knew that our client John Dittmar Ansel had never had anything published in any of the first-string magazines in the United States, either under the name of John Ansel or the name of John Dittmar. I also knew that he had never published any book either of fiction or non-fiction.

I had a friend in the morgue of one of the Los Angeles papers. I went there and got the envelope containing clippings dealing with the murder of Karl Carver Endicott. The Los Angeles papers had given it a pretty good play, setting forth the facts as well as they were known, which wasn't too well.

I got to the bar in time to watch a couple of innings in a baseball game before Elsie's call came through letting me know that Ansel was at the office and that Bertha had been tearing her hair trying to locate me. I waited until one more batter had fanned out.

CHAPTER THREE

As I walked through the office door, the switchboard operator said, "Bertha's frantically trying to get you."

I looked at my watch, raised my eyebrows and said, "I'll go on in."

I walked across the reception office and opened the door of Bertha's private office before the girl at the switchboard had had time to plug in the phone and ring.

Ansel was sitting very erect in the chair, his long legs crossed at the knees. There was a look of reproachful martyrdom on his face.

Bertha Cool batted her eyes at me. Her face was about two shades darker than usual.

"Where the hell have you been?" she asked.

I nodded towards Ansel and said, "Working on our client's case. Why?"

"I couldn't locate you."

"I was out."

"So it seems. You were to have a report for Mr. Ansel."

"I have it."

Ansel raised his dark eyebrows. "Indeed," he murmured.

I went over and shook hands with him. I slid one hip over on the corner of Bertha's desk and said, "I have everything you wanted."

"Well, that's fine," he said. "You mean you've got him located?"

"I know his name," I said. "The man you want is Karl Carver Endicott. He lives at Citrus Grove. He married Elizabeth Flanders six years ago."

I quit talking.

He sat forward on the edge of the chair waiting for me to go on. I lit a cigarette.

The seconds of silence became significant. Bertha started to say something, then realized the silence on my part was deliberate and clamped her lips shut in a thin, straight line. Ansel shifted his position, looked up at me, looked down at the carpet, looked up at me again.

I kept on smoking.

"Well?" Ansel asked, finally.

"That's it," I said, acting surprised. "That's the information you wanted. The name of the man is Karl Carver Endicott. The residence address was Citrus Grove, not right in the city, but outside of the city at an orange grove ranch called the Whippoorwill."

"The Whippoorwill," Ansel repeated vaguely.

I smiled. "That's right. The Whippoorwill."

I went on smoking. Ansel sat in the chair fidgeting.

"Well," I said to Bertha, "I'll be on my way. I'm doing some work on that Russett case, and——"

"But how about me?" Ansel asked.

I turned to look at him in surprise.

"*What* about you? It's finished. It's solved. You wanted the name of good old Karl that you met in Paris. Wanted to know who he was. I got the name for you."

"Well, where is he now?" he asked.

"Good heavens!" I said, "that wasn't what you wanted us to find out. *I* don't know where he is now."

He moistened his lips with the tip of his tongue. "I'd like very much to find out."

"*That* may be quite a job," I said.

"Good heavens! Why?" Bertha blurted. "A man like that wouldn't have moved away without leaving a forwarding address."

"It depends on where he went," I told her significantly.

Bertha caught the look in my eyes and became silent.

"Well, of course, I'd like to know," Ansel said. "I could . . . I hadn't anticipated that you'd get just the name."

"That was all you asked for."

"Perhaps I didn't make my wants clearly understood," he said.

"Perhaps you didn't."

"Well," Bertha snapped impatiently. "Why the hell do you want to fool around with private detectives after you have the man's name and address. Go into a telephone booth. Give him a ring. Drop him a letter. Send him a telegram. Write him a card."

"That's right, Ansel," I said. "You wanted to get in touch with good old Karl whom you met in Paris. He had an idea for a story, remember?"

He ran his hands through his hair and said, "Surely you must have found out *something* about him while you were getting his name."

"Oh, of course," I told him, "but that was just incidental and on the side. What we were supposed to find out was the man's name. You wanted his name. We gave you his name."

"I repeat," Ansel said, "perhaps I didn't express myself clearly."

"You can say that again," I told him. "In case you're interested in the murder, you expressed yourself very, very incompletely."

"I'm *not* interested in the murder," he said. "I merely wanted . . ." His voice suddenly trailed away into dismayed silence.

I grinned at him. "How did you know there'd been a murder, Ansel?"

He tried to answer that question and couldn't. His mouth went through the motions of making sound but gave it up as a bad job.

I could hear Bertha Cool's chair creak as she suddenly came to life behind the desk and leaned forward, scenting financial gain the way a bird dog scents a covey of quail.

"In case you are interested in learning about the murder, Ansel," I told him, "you made several very important mistakes. One of them is that you neglected to tell me the principal suspect was described as a tall, rather slender man with dark hair, dark eyes, and long artistic fingers. A taxi driver is supposed to be able to identify that man.

"And you made the mistake of not telling me what I was up against so I could have covered my back trail. As it was, I went out in the open without making any attempt to cover up and by this time the authorities know that the firm of Cool & Lam is interested in the Karl Endicott case. Since the police have nasty, sceptical minds, they wouldn't believe that my interest in the case was purely for the purpose of locating quote good old Karl unquote who gave you an idea for quote a story unquote while you were in Paris. They would naturally think that we were interested in some angle of the murder, and, within a very short time, the police are going to want to know *why* we are interested.

"The third mistake you made was in not giving us an address where you could be reached so that when I found out what we were up against I could have warned you and told you not to come to the office.

"However, since all those mistakes have been made you'll have to take your chances. Next time you employ detectives tell them what you want. In the meantime, give us fifty bucks."

"But ... but ..." Ansel said, sputtering like a cold motorcycle motor, "you're jumping at conclusions."

"Detectives sometimes do that," I told him.

He squirmed around in the chair. "I'm sorry," he said, at length.

"Well," I said, "we've done our job. We got you the information you *said* you wanted. We're not mind readers. Give my partner the fifty bucks you owe us."

I started for the door.

"Hey, wait a minute!" Bertha said. "Where are you going?"

"Out!" I told her.

Ansel sat there looking very much nonplussed.

I walked out of the office, went down to the parking lot, got in the agency heap, started the motor and waited.

It was nearly fifteen minutes before Ansel came out. He

looked over his shoulder apprehensively a couple of times, but seemed reassured when he found no one appeared to be taking any interest in him.

As it turned out he had his car parked in the same parking lot where we kept ours. I had a good look as he drove out. It was a serviceable, nondescript Chevy, four year old, and the licence number was AWY 421.

I followed him for a ways. He played it about half-smart. After he got out to where there wasn't so much traffic, he started cutting figure eights around four block squares, obviously looking in his rear view mirror to see if anyone was taking an interest in what he was doing.

I quit following him, drove on down the main boulevard half a mile, parked on a side street and waited.

He must have gone through a lot of complicated manœuvres to shake off any pursuit, because it was a good twenty minutes before I saw his car sailing along down the main boulevard.

By that time he had convinced himself no one was following him, and it was a cinch to drop in behind him.

I trailed him to a bungalow out on Betward Drive.

He parked the car and I curbed the agency heap half a block down the street.

I saw him get out and enter the bungalow.

When he hadn't come out after thirty minutes, I drove back to the office.

The girls had gone home. Bertha was sitting there alone waiting.

"Where the hell have you been?"

"Out."

"What's the idea of getting up and leaving a client in the middle of a conference?"

"We found out everything we agreed to find out for him."

"So what?" Bertha said. "If you were half as brainy as you're supposed to be, you'd have realized that merely because we'd finished one job is no sign he wouldn't give us another."

"I felt certain he was going to *offer* us another," I said.

"What do you mean by that?" she asked.

"He wants us to find out if it's safe for him to come back."

"What do you mean, safe for him to come back?"

I said, "A cab-driver by the name of Nickerson took a fare out to Endicott's house the night of the murder. Nickerson described the fare as being a tall, slender man with dark eyes, a man in his late twenties, who was carrying a brief case. Shortly before he got to the Endicott house, he opened the brief case, took out a gun and put it in his hip pocket. The taxi driver thought it was a stick-up. He was watching in the rear-view mirror. It wasn't a stick-up. The fare kept on going to the Endicott ranch, paid off the cab, gave the driver a dollar tip and walked up to the front door. The cab-driver went on about his business. Next day he told the police."

"Nickerson, eh?" Bertha asked.

I nodded.

"The only witness?"

"He's the only one the police ever said anything about. There was a banker in the living-room, a chap named Hale. He had a business appointment with Endicott."

"What happened?" Bertha asked.

"It was a night when the servants were all gone. Endicott had gone through a marital crisis with his wife a short time before and his wife had packed up a suitcase, taken her car and driven away. Fortunately for her the wife stopped at a gasoline station in Citrus Grove. It was a station where she had a charge account and she had the car filled up with gas and checked for oil. The attendant remembers the time because he was just closing up the place when she drove in.

"Hale said the doorbell rang. Endicott excused himself and went to the door. Hale heard some man engage in a brief conversation with Endicott, then he heard steps in the hallway, heard voices, and after a minute or so the sound of a shot from upstairs.

"Hale ran upstairs and it took him a moment to locate Endicott who was in an upstairs bedroom. Endicott was lying on the floor in a pool of blood. He was stone dead. A .38 bullet had smashed into the back of his head."

Bertha's little, greedy eyes were glittering with intense concentration.

"What about the cab-driver?" she asked.

"The cab-driver knows that the man reached the house a minute or so before nine o'clock, because he went off duty at nine. He was seven minutes late turning in his cab at the station. The witness Hale places the shooting at exactly nine o'clock, and the service station man at Citrus Grove says Mrs. Endicott drove in, then left his station at exactly nine o'clock. He was just closing up.

"Mrs. Endicott drove to San Diego. No one knew where she was. Later on, she told police she knew nothing about the murder until the next morning when she heard it on the radio. She returned for the funeral. Endicott left no will. His wife inherited everything. There were no other heirs.

"After a few months Mrs. Endicott settled down in the Whippoorwill, the Endicott home. She seldom goes out and is reported to be living the life of a recluse.

"Hale has told intimate friends that shortly before the murder Endicott had confided in him his wife had left him for good, that Endicott was pretty well broken up and exceedingly nervous.

"The police have the idea Endicott was paying blackmail to someone and that the person who killed him may have been the blackmailer."

"How come?" Bertha asked.

"Endicott had drawn twenty thousand dollars in cash that morning. It was the third time he had drawn large amounts of cash within a period of three months. The other times he had drawn ten thousand. He had told Hale he was expecting a visitor who would take only a few moments."

"Fry me for an oyster!" Bertha Cool said. "Ten grand a month! That's *some* blackmail!"

"That's some blackmail," I agreed.

Bertha thought things over.

"Did you let him sell you a bill of goods or are we in the clear?" I asked her.

"What the hell do you mean, a 'bill of goods'?" Bertha asked.

I said, "He matches the description of the guy described by the taxi driver, the one who called on Endicott a few minutes before the shot was fired. Police thing this guy was the blackmailer and that Endicott issued some sort of an ultimatum that he was through paying."

"Well?" Bertha asked.

I said, "What would you do if you were a blackmailer, Bertha? Suppose you had a sucker who was good for ten grand a month. Would you kill him?"

"Hell, no!" Bertha said. "I'd take out life insurance on him, and hire a bodyguard to keep him under observation and see he didn't walk in front of any street-cars."

"Exactly," I told her.

Bertha thought things over. "Then if it wasn't for that taxi driver they wouldn't have any case at all."

"Probably," I said. "However, you never can tell about the police. They're pretty damn smart."

"They sure are," Bertha agreed. "Do you know the cab-driver's first name?"

"An unusual name."

"What was it?"

I pulled out a notebook. "Drude. D-r-u-d-e. Drude Nickerson," I said.

A smile twisted the corners of Bertha's mouth. "Someday, Donald," she said, "you'll admit that while you have brains when it comes to solving a case, Bertha has brains when it comes to raking in the cash."

"What do you mean?" I asked.

Bertha opened the drawer in her desk and pulled out five new, unfolded, one-hundred-dollar bills.

"What's that?" I asked.

"A retainer," she said.

"For what?"

"For information that we've got already."

"What do you mean?"

"How did you get the information about the murder?"

I said, "When I knew we'd been suckered into a deal we probably didn't want, I ran through the newspapers in order to find out what we might be up against."

"Well, you've got the information," Bertha said. "Take a look at this."

She handed me a newspaper clipping which had been cut from the obituary column of one of the papers.

I read it. "*Nickerson, Drude, beloved husband of Maria Nickerson. Killed in automobile accident near Susanville, California. Private funeral, Susanville Undertaking Parlours. No flowers.*"

"How nice!" I said. "What does that have to do with the five-hundred-dollar retainer?"

"We're to find out if this dead guy is the same Nickerson who drove the cab to the Endicott house. We get five hundred bucks more when we've finished the investigation, and we get a reasonable allowance for expenses. Go to it, Donald!"

"You shouldn't have taken it, Bertha."

"What the hell do you mean, I shouldn't have taken it?" Bertha screamed. "There's five hundred perfectly good legal bucks. We can use that lettuce on our income tax. Don't tell me we don't want it."

"It's loaded with dynamite."

"All right," Bertha said, "it's loaded with dynamite. So what? All the man wants is an answer to one simple question: whether Drude Nickerson is the cab-driver."

I looked at my watch, "Well," I said, "let's hope we still have time."

"Time for what?" Bertha snapped.

"Time to investigate the murder of William Desmond Taylor," I said. "You may remember that case. It was in 1921. One of the most famous of the unsolved Hollywood murders."

For once I had Bertha off her base.

"One or the other of us is completely nuts," she yelled. I opened the door.

"Come back here!" Bertha was screaming at the top of her voice. "Come back here, you little runt, and——"

The closing outer door of the office shut off the noise. I made time to the public library and started digging into the files of the murder of William Desmond Taylor.

CHAPTER FOUR

THE death of William Desmond Taylor was a Hollywood classic.

Taylor had been a famous Hollywood director, back in the days of the silent pictures.

When, early one morning in 1921, William Desmond Taylor's butler and general handyman opened the door of the unit in the bungalow court where Taylor was living and found him lying dead on the floor, it started a chain of events which had unexpected repercussions.

It was found that William Desmond Taylor was not William Desmond Taylor at all, but one William Deane Tanner who had mysteriously disappeared from New York some years before. The biographical data which surrounded the famous motion-picture director was as fictitious as the plots he had concocted in the silent days of the pictures.

Stories circulated around Hollywood and found their way into the newspapers about a mysterious woman's silk nightie which, according to rumour, the butler found neatly folded in an upstairs bureau drawer. The butler very carefully refolded the nightie in a certain manner only to find that, at regular intervals, the sheer silken garment would have been carefully refolded in an entirely different pattern.

The names of motion-picture actresses, famous names of the day, flitted in and out of the case with bizarre statements, explanations, comments and rumours, fully in keeping with the exaggerated gestures of the silent pictures.

In those days, it is to be remembered, an actor dashing in pursuit of someone who was only two jumps ahead would run to a corner of the set, come to a dead stop, invariably look in the wrong direction, shade his eyes with his hand in order to signify that he was looking, then turn in the opposite direction, again shade his eyes, stab his finger in a pointing gesture to indicate unmistakably that his quarry was "going that-a-way" and then from a standing start resume the pursuit until the next corner of the set was reached, when the pantomime would be repeated.

The investigation of the murder of William Desmond Taylor followed a similar pattern.

I made copious notes.

When the library closed, I knocked off for the night, with two shorthand books filled with notes.

Wednesday morning I went once more to the newspaper files in the morgue.

Bertha Cool was just going out to lunch as I came in.

"You've been to Susanville?" she asked.

"I'm going."

"Going?" she said. "My God! You're supposed to have been on your way long ago. Our client rang up and I told him you were already up there."

"That's fine," I said.

"What the hell *have* you been doing?" Bertha blazed at me.

"Getting some insurance," I said.

"Insurance?"

I nodded.

"For what?"

"To keep us from losing our licence," I told her.

"When are you starting?" Bertha asked, too exasperated to ask for particulars.

"Now," I told her. "I take a plane to Reno; then I'm renting a car at Reno and driving to Susanville."

Bertha glared at me angrily. "When will you get to Susanville?"

"It all depends," I told her.

She said, "Our client is on pins and needles. He's telephoned twice. He wanted to know if you'd taken off. I told him you had."

"That's fine. As long as he feels we're on the job, he'll be satisfied."

Bertha's face darkened. "Why the hell do you need to take out insurance when we're working on a dead open-and-shut case?"

"Because it's dead open-and-shut."

"What do you mean?"

I said, "The police would like to clean up the Endicott murder. They have one witness, a taxi driver by the name of Drude Nickerson. He's their case. All of a sudden the obituary column reports the death of Drude Nickerson up in Susanville. It's private. No flowers. You'd naturally think the body would be shipped back here to Citrus Grove and that the funeral would be held there."

Bertha blinked that over.

"I'll be seeing you," I told her, and started for the door.

"Pickle me for a beet!" Bertha said under her breath as I opened the door.

CHAPTER FIVE

It was late afternoon when I pulled in to Susanville. I located myself in a motel and registered under my true name, giving the address of the agency.

I looked up the Susanville Undertaking Parlours.

"You have a body here—Nickerson?" I asked.

The man at the desk sized me up carefully, then made a show of looking through some records and a card index.

"That's right."

"Can you give me his first name?"

"Drude," he said. "D-r-u-d-e."

"Know anything about the man's background or anything?"

"It was a coroner's case," he said. "Injuries on the highway."

"When's the funeral?" I asked.

"Private."

"I know it's private, but when?"

"It hasn't been decided yet."

"Could I see the body?"

"It's a closed casket case. Who are you?"

"The name," I said, "is Lam, Donald Lam, from Los Angeles."

"A relative?"

"No. I'm interested."

"What's your interest?"

"Just checking. Nickerson lived in Citrus Grove. How come they aren't having the funeral there?"

"Don't ask me."

"The coroner handled the case?"

"That's right."

"I'll get in touch with the coroner."

"Do that."

"How about this man's clothes?" I asked. "I take it he had identification. Could I take a look at his driver's licence?"

"I'd have to get permission."

"How long would it take?"

"Not long."

The man picked up a telephone, dialled a number, said, "There's a Donald Lam here from Los Angeles inquiring about Drude Nickerson, wants to take a look at the man's driving licence and stuff that was in the clothes, wants to be sure of the identification, making inquiries. What'll I do?"

The man listened for a moment, then said, "Okay."

He hung up the phone, and said, "A representative of the

coroner is coming right over. He'll show you what you want to see if you can give him a reason."

"I'll give him a reason," I said.

I waited for about two and a half minutes. I tried to get the man at the desk in conversation, but he'd quit talking. He made a great show of doing some paper work.

The door opened and three men walked in. They had LAW stamped all over them.

The man at the desk motioned towards me with his thumb. The three men moved in on me.

"Okay," one of them said, flashing a badge. "I'm the sheriff here. What's your interest in the Nickerson case?"

"I'm making an investigation."

"Why?"

"I'm a detective."

"The hell you are."

"That's right."

"Let's take a look."

I showed him my credentials.

The sheriff looked at the taller of the two men, said, "All right, Lam, this is the second pass you've made on this case. This gentleman here is the sheriff of Orange County."

"How are you?" I said. "Glad to know you."

The Orange County sheriff nodded curtly, made no move to put out his hand. "What were you doing checking newspapers in Citrus Grove yesterday, asking about the Endicott case?"

"I was looking up the facts."

"All right," the local sheriff said. "I think you'd better come with us."

They moved in, one on each side, and escorted me out to an automobile.

They took me direct to a private residence. I assumed it was that of the local sheriff.

The sheriff from Orange County took charge. He was rather a nice individual, but he was determined and he was mad.

"You can't pull a run-around like that with the law," he said. "You're a licensed member of a detective agency. This is murder."

"Sure, it's murder," I said.

"Now, you went down to the newspaper in Citrus Grove and started messing around looking up dope on the Endicott murder, didn't you?"

"No."

"Don't lie to me, because we have the information that——"

I said, "If you get your information straight, you'll find that I was looking up Endicott's marriage."

The men exchanged glances.

"Get the newspaper on the phone," I told them. "I'll pay for

20

the call. You'll find out that I didn't show the faintest interest in the murder at that time. I was looking up the marriage."

The sheriff waved the matter to one side. "All right. No need to put through the telephone call. We'll take your word for it. You were looking up the marriage. *Why* were you looking up the marriage?"

"Because I already had everything on the murder."

"You admit that?"

"Sure, I admit it."

"You'd been looking up the murder?"

"Of course I'd been looking up the murder."

"Well, now that's a lot better. That's just a hell of a lot better. Now *why* were you looking up the murder? What's it to you? What do you know about the case?"

"I know everything that the police have given the newspapers about the case," I said. "The death of this fellow Nickerson gives it a swell angle. I'm looking up a whole series of unsolved murder cases in the South-west. I'm going to write a regional book. I don't know whether to call it *Southern Californian Murders*, or what to call it."

"Don't expect us to fall for a line like that," the sheriff said.

"Why not? There's money in that stuff. You can sell it to some of the magazines that specialize in true crime stories, and then you can bring it out in book form.

"In case you folks are interested, I put in a lot of time yesterday and a lot of time today investigating the William Desmond Taylor murder. Now *there's* a story!"

"Yeah, it's been written up about seventeen thousand times," the Orange County sheriff said.

"Not the way I'm going to write it."

"What's the way you're going to write it?"

"I'm not going to blab *that* around and have some other writer beat me to it."

"What writing have you ever done?"

"None."

"Don't make me laugh," the local sheriff said.

"A man has to begin sometime."

The Orange County sheriff took over. "Yeah, you start in spending a lot of money for travelling expenses. *You* want to begin at the top," he said sarcastically.

"Well," I said, "*you* began at the top."

"What do you mean by that crack?"

"You had quite a story about the Endicott murder in one of the true crime magazines. Had *you* ever done any writing before?"

"I didn't write it," he said. "That was ghosted. They used my name."

21

"Well," I told him, "I think I've got a talent for writing, and, because of my position as a private detective, I think I can get the inside track on some of these stories and get some red-hot stuff."

I grabbed up my brief case and said, "Here, take a look. I have no objection to showing you the notes I have on the William Desmond Taylor case. I'm not going to tell you my angle of approach on that case, how I'm going to treat it, but you can take a look at the notes."

They took a good, long look at the notes. They went through every notebook in the brief case. They exchanged glances. They were puzzled and angry.

"Why did you come to Susanville?" the deputy asked me.

"To check on Nickerson."

"Why?"

"Because if Nickerson is dead, you're never going to find the murderer in that Endicott case."

"Don't be too sure," the Orange County sheriff said.

I said, "Perhaps if his conscience gets to bothering him and he confesses, you'll nab him. Otherwise you don't stand a chance."

"Why did you want to see the body?" the Susanville sheriff asked.

"I wanted to see if I could get an exclusive photograph of the body in the coffin."

"Well, you can't."

"All right. I want to get some photographs of the accident, where he sustained fatal injuries. I want to do some research work."

The sheriff shook his head.

"Why not?"

"Because we don't want you to."

"Why don't you want me to?"

The Orange County sheriff said, "Because we're baiting— because we don't want you messing around and interfering with some work we're doing."

The resident deputy said hastily, "We're still working on the case, and we don't want any outsiders messing around."

"I can hunt up the records on the accident and take a look at the wrecked cars and get a photograph," I said. "It's a red-hot story."

"No, it isn't. The newspapers are co-operating, and *you're* going to co-operate."

I became petulant. "I put out some of my good hard-earned money getting up here to get some pictures."

"Where's your camera?"

"I'm going to rent one. I'm going to cover all of my cases with rented cameras. Then I can tell the kind of camera I want to buy. But I don't want to tie a lot of money up in a camera at the beginning of my writing career."

The Susanville sheriff said, "Let's talk things over, boys."

They got up and went through a door. "You stay here, Lam," he said.

I waited for about five minutes.

They came back. The sheriff of Orange County said, "You work in Los Angeles?"

"That's right."

"Who do you know on the police there?"

"Frank Sellers of Homicide."

"Stick around," the resident deputy said. "We're putting through a call."

He placed the call, hung up.

The men looked at each other as they waited for the call. I could feel the accusation in their attitudes.

Suddenly the telephone shattered the silence with a shrill ringing.

The sheriff said, "That'll be Frank Sellers," picked up the telephone, said, "Hello," and then from the sudden change in the expression on his face I knew something had happened.

"What's the name?" he asked. "How do you spell it? How's that? Give it to me again."

He picked up a pencil and wrote on the top paper of a memo pad, then said, "Okay, what's her first name? ... Her own car? ... Okay, what's the licence number? That's in California?

"Can you stall her along? ... Oh, ten minutes.... Well, we'll work as fast as we can.... We're waiting on a long distance call to Los Angeles now.... Okay, do the best you can.... Well, if you *have* to. Call back if you have to."

He hung up the phone, glanced significantly at the others, picked the top sheet off the memo pad, folded it, put it in his pocket, looked at his watch, started to say something.

The telephone rang again.

He scooped up the receiver, said, "Hello," and the expression on his face told me he had Sellers on the line.

He identified himself and said, "We've got a private detective up here, name of Donald Lam. Do you know anything about him?"

The receiver made squawking noises.

"He's messing around in a case. He says his only interest is in getting material for an article he intends to write. It's a case we don't want anyone lousing up for a while. How do we handle him?"

Again the receiver made squawking noises.

"Give me some more dope," the sheriff said.

Sellers must have talked for about three minutes.

"Okay," the sheriff said.

He hung up the phone and turned to me. His voice was more kindly. "Sellers says you're one hell of a smart operator, that you'll protect a client all the way, and that we can't believe a word you say."

"That's nice," I told him.

"Sellers also said that if you give your word you'll stay with it."

"That's *if*," I said.

"That's right, *if*."

There was a short period of silence.

"How did you come here?"

"I rented a car from Reno."

"All right, Lam. You're free to start back."

"I don't want to start back."

"Sellers gave me a message for you. As a personal favour to him, you're to start back. Sellers said that if you're representing a client you won't go back. He says that if you stick around it will mean you're working on this case for a client. He says that if you're just free lancing for a story you'll come back as a personal favour to him."

I managed to move over to sit on the corner of the table by the telephone and make it seem I was trying to make up my mind. I put my right hand behind me and rested my weight on it, and when I made certain my body concealed my right hand from them, I eased it over to the container which held the sheets of memo paper by the telephone and pulled off the top sheet. This was the one that had been directly underneath the sheet on which the sheriff had done the writing.

I folded the sheet of paper into halves, palmed it, and as I straightened slipped my right hand into my trousers pocket.

They were watching my face and none of them attached the slightest significance to my motions.

"Well?" the sheriff asked.

"Let me think it over."

"You've thought it over."

"Sellers is a nice guy. I hate to disappoint him."

"He says you're too damned smart to be trusted."

"That was nice of him."

"I thought so."

"That makes sense," I said.

"Sellers said it would."

"All right," I told him, picking up the brief case. "I hate to waste the money but I'm starting back."

The Orange County sheriff said, "I'm not entirely satisfied with this, fellows."

"Neither am I," the third man said.

I put eagerness into my voice. "Want me to stick around for a day or two?" I asked. "Perhaps by that time I can have a *real* story."

"No," the Orange County sheriff said, "on second thought we want you the hell out of here and we want you out now. You'll have an hour to get started. We'll show you the right road out of town in case you aren't on your way by then."

"There's no trouble finding the road out of town."

"There might be for you."

"I hate to be run out like this."

"We know you do, but it's a personal favour for Sergeant Sellers unless of course you're up here representing a client."

I told them good-bye, walked out, got in my car and slipped the piece of paper from my pocket. There were faint indentations on it. I took my knife, cut the point of a soft pencil to powdered graphite, rubbed the black powder over the paper with my finger and soon had a legible imprint of what the sheriff had written down: "*Stella Karis, 6825 Morehead Street, Los Angeles. Licence No. JYH 328.*"

I went to my motel. The manager said the sheriff had phoned to move the things out of my unit and give me my money back.

I opined that was real thoughtful of the sheriff.

I drove down to the second boulevard stop, parked my car and waited. It was dark now but street lights enabled me to read licence numbers.

An hour passed.

I was ready to give up and was just starting my motor when my car came along, a Ford, licence number JYH 328.

A young woman was driving it and when I fell in behind her I realized she was breaking all speed laws. I tagged along behind for a ways.

Suddenly the red brake lights blazed on in the car in front. The driver pulled over to the side of the road and stopped. The door on the driver's side opened. I saw a beautiful pair of legs, a flash of skirt, and then she was standing in front of me on the highway.

I slid rubber getting to a stop.

She didn't budge.

I opened the door and got out.

"Now just what do you think *you're* doing?" she demanded.

"Me?" I said. "I'm going to Reno."

"Yes, I know you're going to Reno, but you're afraid you might get lost so you want a pilot car to keep ahead of you and you've been tagging me for the last twenty miles. Now suppose you just get that car of yours going and keep it going until you get to Reno.

"However, if, as I suspect is the case, you're a local minion of the law making certain that I'm leaving the county, you can go

25

back to Susanville and tell them that I don't want any part of the place."

I said, "I'm not connected with the Susanville law. I'm on my own. And if you don't mind my saying so, a good-looking young woman like you could get into serious trouble stopping her car to find out who had been following her for the last twenty miles."

"That's right!" she blazed at me. "I mind your saying so. It was so nice of you to think of it first. Now get going, and keep going! How many of you are in the car?"

"Just me."

She walked over to the car and took a look.

"All right, go on ahead."

"I might have something in the line of information that you could use." I said. "My name's Donald Lam."

"I don't care a hoot what your name is. As far as I'm concerned you can get lost."

I climbed in the car and pulled ahead of her. I rolled on down the road about five miles until I found a cross-road, then brought my car to a stop, backed into the cross-road, switched off my lights and the ignition, and waited.

Headlights appeared down the road. I could hear the whine of tyres on the highway. A car rocketed on past. It wasn't the car the girl had been driving.

This was out in the wilderness and cars were relatively few and far between. I sat behind the steering wheel and waited.

Another car rocketed past. That wasn't the girl's car.

Five minutes after that another car came along rather slowly. That was the girl's car.

I gave her about five minutes' start, then gave my car the gas. I overtook her, went tearing on past, got over a little rise in the road and slowed almost to a stop. When I saw her headlights in my rearview mirror I kept going. I kept ahead of her for another twenty or thirty miles before she got the idea. Then she came barreling up with her headlights on high blazing into my rearview mirror and crowded me off the road. I stopped and she stopped.

She got out of the car and walked over to the window.

"What did you say your name was?"

"Donald Lam."

"What do you do, Mr. Lam?"

"I'm a private detective."

"How interesting! You don't have one of your cards do you?"

I gave her one of my cards.

"Could I see your driving licence, just to check?"

I showed her the driving licence.

She put the card in her purse. "All right," she said, "now I know who you are, and if you keep annoying me on the road I'm going to have you arrested when we get to Reno."

"Arrested for what?"

"Arrested for annoying me and for a few other assorted misdemeanours."

I smiled and said, "This is a public highway. I haven't annoyed you in any way. You're going to Reno. I'm going to Reno."

"You mean there's nothing I can do?" she asked.

"Not a thing unless I try to flirt with you, and I haven't done that. I haven't annoyed you. I've followed the letter of the law as far as driving is concerned and——"

She reached up her left hand, hooked it in the neck of her blouse and jerked.

The fabric gave a rip. She lifted the hem of her skirt, took the cloth in both hands and pulled. For a minute she couldn't make it, then the hem gave way and the skirt ripped halfway up to the waist.

"Ever hear of criminal assault?" she asked.

I nodded.

"All right, that's what you've done. Have any idea what the penalty for that is?"

I shook my head.

"I don't either," she said, "but there's a very nice, homey, little penitentiary down at Carson City and that's where you're going. You asked for this, Mr. Lam. Now you're going to get it. I tried to be nice about it, but you had to be the smart guy.

"You followed me along the road. I stopped to protest. You grabbed me and threw me down by the side of the road. I struggled to free myself. Finally the lights of another car showed up and I screamed for help. You let go of me and I dashed to my car and managed to keep ahead of you all the way into Reno."

"You aren't in Nevada yet," I told her. "You're still in California."

She didn't answer that, just turned, raced back to her car, jumped in behind the steering wheel, slammed the door and took off from there fast.

I tried to pass her and couldn't. She was driving like the devil and whenever I'd try to get by she'd swing over to the centre of the road.

We were doing eighty when the red spotlight blazed on behind me. The officer waved me off to the side of the road.

There was nothing for it. I swung over to the side of the road.

The traffic officer pulled alongside. "Follow me." he ordered, "but don't try to keep up with me. I'm stopping that car up ahead."

He took off with a roar. I gave the bus all it would take. I saw the red light on the girl's car, heard the scream of the siren softened by distance.

The girl gave him a run for it. I had to step on it to keep up with him. He finally got her crowded off the road just before we came to the state line, about fifteen miles out of Reno.

The officer was mad.

I came up behind, parked my car, got out and walked over to where the officer was standing.

I raised my voice. "You should have given me an opportunity to explain back there. I tried to catch your attention."

He whirled to me. "You get the hell back there and mind your own business," he blazed. "I told you to take it easy. I was going ninety miles an hour catching up to this car and you were right behind me."

"Sure, I was right behind you!" I shouted at him. "I was trying to stop you. What the hell did you think I was trying to do?"

The belligerency in my voice caused him to size me up, taking a new slant on the situation.

"Someone assaulted this girl," I said. "We were dashing ahead looking for the law. If you'd only stopped and listened to what I was trying to tell you, you could have caught that carload of hoodlums going towards Susanville. But not you! You were so damned intent on giving orders that you wouldn't listen."

He cocked his head to one side.

"What's this you're talking about?" he asked.

"About a carload of hoodlums that crowded this girl off the road and tried to assault her. Heavens knows what would have happened if I hadn't come along! Take a look at her. Look at her clothes."

The officer said, "What are you giving me? She's drunk. She was driving all over the road. You were trying to pass her and she was swinging out in front of you. You were chasing her and——"

"She's emotionally upset," I said. "She's hysterical. She was trying to get to some place where she could telephone the road patrol."

"I had my siren on," he said, "and she didn't pay a damn bit of attention."

I moved up to the car. "Did you hear his siren, miss?" I asked.

She started to cry. "I guess I heard it but I was too afraid to stop. I thought it was those boys coming back."

I said to the officer by way of explanation, "That's the way they got her to stop in the first place. One of the kids made a sound like a siren. It was a pretty good imitation. She pulled off to the side of the road and stopped and they dragged her out of the car."

"Where were you?" he asked.

"I must have been just about five miles behind," I said. "They crowded me off the road as they went by."

"What kind of a car?"

"A '52 Buick, black sedan."

"How many people?"

"Four," I said. "All kids. One had a T-shirt and tan leather jacket, another a suède blazer, a third a buttoned sweater and the fourth had a sports coat and shirt with no tie, the collar on the outside of the sports coat."

"Get their licence number?"

"I did," I admitted sheepishly, "and then in the excitement I forgot it. I didn't have a chance to write it down. I was trying to keep this young woman in sight and see that nothing happened to her."

The officer was undecided for a moment. He said, "That sounds like a gang we've been having trouble with. One of the kids a tall blond?"

"Yeah," I said. "The one in the blazer. Looked like a basket-ball player."

"About nineteen or twenty? Something over six feet?" he asked.

"I'm not certain," I said. "They got out of there in a hurry when I brought my car to a stop."

"Just you by yourself, and you were going to take on these four hoodlums?" he asked.

"They didn't know I was alone in the car," I said. "I have a gun that I could have used if I had to."

"*You've* got a gun?"

"That's right."

"Let's take a look at your permit."

I showed him my credentials.

He thought things over for a while, then turned to the woman. "Let's see your driving licence."

She gave it to him.

"Stella Karis, eh? Okay, what do you want to do? Do you want to make a complaint?"

She said, "I did, but I don't. Why should I get my name in the papers, after all I've been through?"

The officer said, "That's not going to help the next girl who gets waylaid on the road, Miss Karis."

I said, "If they interview you, Miss Karis, you don't need to tell them anything about the officer chasing you instead of the carload of juveniles."

His eyes narrowed. "Nineteen-fifty-two Buick, you say?"

"Uh-huh."

"Black sedan?"

"Either black or such a dark colour that it looked black. As I get the story, they passed her once, then dropped behind her and let her pass them. Then they passed her again, studying the car, then dropped way behind and the third time they made a noise like a siren. When she slowed to a stop they dragged her out of the car, and——"

"Okay, okay," the officer said. "But you should have remembered the licence number."

"If you'd listened to me when I was yelling at you," I told him, "there was still time for you to have overtaken this car."

"Maybe," he mumbled, "but that didn't give her an excuse to be driving all over the road."

"She's emotionally upset."

"Okay, okay," he said. "I'll go on in to the checking station and telephone for a roadblock. Those hoodlums probably turned off, but there's a chance we may catch them. We've been having trouble with that gang. Could you identify the car, Lam?"

"I didn't see any distinctive marks but I know there were four of these young punks and it was a '52 Buick, black sedan. That's about the best I can give you except that I could identify that tall blond kid, or I think I could. And perhaps the chunky fellow with the low black hairline. The rest of them I didn't see so good."

"Okay, I'll go on in and phone."

The officer strode back to his car, jumped in, and whipped by us like a streak.

I stood by the window of Stella Karis's car.

Abruptly she began to laugh. She said, "Donald, did you really think I was going to turn you in?"

"You tore up some good clothes."

"I didn't want you messing in my business. I've found that's a perfect way to get rid of any man who makes a nuisance of himself. It literally scares them out of their wits. Now I've got to get into my suitcase and put on some fresh clothes."

"Better wait until you get across the state line," I said. "We pass the checking station right up the line here."

"Okay, you lead the way."

I told her, "Okay. Now how about dinner in Reno?"

She laughed. "You're one fast worker," she said. "What's your game?"

"I'm checking up on Drude Nickerson, the cab-driver," I said. "They ran me out of town."

Her eyes got wide. "Is *that* what you were doing?"

I nodded.

"You've got yourself a dinner date," she said. "Know a good motel?"

I nodded.

"Lead the way."

The traffic officer was telephoning from the checking station as we went by. I waved at him and he gave us a casual signal with his hand. I gathered that he didn't want publicity any more than we did. I also had the disturbing thought that he might be doing a lot of thinking and after he got done with his thinking the results might not be so good.

We crossed the state line and about five miles out of town I pulled to a stop.

Stella Karis stopped her car behind mine, got out a suitcase, opened it, walked around on the side of the car that was away from the road.

It didn't take her sixty seconds to get out of the torn blouse and skirt and into other clothes. She came around the car to look me over.

"Are you kidding or are you on the square?" she asked.

"I'm on the square," I told her.

"You're interested in Drude Nickerson?"

"Yes."

"Why?"

"For reasons that I can't tell you and couldn't tell the local law. They told me to get out of town."

"What's your opinion?" she asked.

"About you?"

"Don't be silly. About Nickerson."

"I can't give you any opinion at the present time."

"Why not?"

"Various reasons."

"Do you mean you don't have an opinion or you can't give me one?"

"I can't give you one."

"My!" she said. "You're helpful."

"I'm working," I told her.

"Very well," she said. "You asked me for a dinner date. You have the dinner date. I am also going to worm the information I want out of you."

"How?" I asked.

"Wiles," she said. "Seductive charm. Perhaps liquor."

"What's your interest in Nickerson?" I asked.

"I haven't any."

"Don't make me laugh."

She said, "Lead the way to a motel. Don't try any funny stuff when it comes to registering. You get a single and I'll get a single and I hope they're far apart. Give me twenty minutes to freshen up, then come tap gently on the door of my cabin and we'll go to dinner. Are you on an expense account?"

"Yes."

"Okay," she said, "you buy."

31

"I buy," I told her.

I got in the car and led the way into Reno, picked out a good motel. It was filled up. I went to another one. It was filled up. I walked back to Stella Karis's car.

"We may have trouble getting accommodation," I said.

"Okay," she told me. "We'll do the best we can."

"Suppose we can't get two separate cabins," I said. "Could we——?"

"We could not," she interrupted.

"Could we," I asked, "stay in separate courts?"

She smiled. "I misjudged you, Donald. We could."

"All right," I said. "We'll keep trying."

The next motel was a good-looking modern place. It had two singles.

The manager looked us over rather sceptically, but gave us keys to the single cabins.

"Twenty minutes," she said.

"Going to do any telephoning?" I asked her.

She smiled. "I might. How about you?"

"I'm sending a wire."

"Okay," she said. "Twenty minutes."

I went to my room and composed a wire to Bertha.

"Present situation purely horticultural. Just another plant. No reason to get excited but don't think our client wants to add a plant of this commonplace variety to his collection. Regards. Donald."

CHAPTER SIX

I TAPPED gently on the door of Stella Karis's unit of the motel.

"Who is it?" she asked.

"Donald," I said.

"Come on in."

I opened the door. She was seated in front of a mirror at the dressing-table.

She turned slowly to look over her bare shoulder at me and lowered her long lashes. "Hello, Donald," she said seductively.

I knew damn well it had been carefully rehearsed, but if it was effect she was after, the rehearsal was worth it.

She got slowly to her feet and came towards me.

She was wearing a semi-formal creation that left her shoulders bare and showed her figure to great advantage.

Seeing her dolled up, I became increasingly aware of her curves, of her cool, competent eyes with their long lashes, the supple way in which she moved, the long, artistic fingers which rested lightly on my arm.

"Donald, you'll forgive me, won't you?"

"For what?"

"For thinking you were the local law sent to chaperone me across the state line and make sure I didn't turn back. I was so damn mad . . . well, I thought I'd pull that torn clothing act on you and panic you into a disorderly retreat."

"That," I told her, "was taking an unfair advantage of your sex."

"Everything about sex is unfair," she said. "Even nature is unfair about sex. Sex gives both sides an unfair advantage—otherwise I wouldn't be with you right now."

"I think you need a drink," I told her.

"I think I do, too." She gave me a wrap. I held it for her and we went out on the town. I bought her two cocktails before dinner, and she insisted on a third, watching me to see whether she could loosen me up that way. We had a nice dinner. We played roulette. We played twenty-one. We shot craps. We played the slot machines. I was about eight dollars ahead, and she'd cleaned up something over a hundred and fifty, all without any great trace of excitement.

It was about one-thirty when I drove her back to the motel.

"Coming in?" she asked.

"It's late," I said.

"What are you afraid of?"

"You."

"How come?"

"You have such a delightful habit of tearing your clothes off and calling the law."

"Oh," she said, "I only do that with my cheaper working clothes. When I'm wearing these clothes, you're perfectly safe."

I went in.

She sat on the davenport. I sat down beside her.

"All right," I told her. "This is the showdown. I know your name. I know your licence number. I'm a detective. I can look you up. That takes time. It takes money. Why don't you tell me?"

She said, "I know your name. I have your business card. I know your address. I know your telephone number. Look, Donald, is there any chance that you're in this thing investigating the murder of Karl Carver Endicott?"

"I told you I couldn't discuss my reasons for being up here."

She looked at me thoughtfully and said, "Drude Nickerson is crooked."

"The whole city's crooked," I told her.

"Susanville?"

"Citrus Grove."

"Donald, if your interest is in the Endicott murder case, we might be able to help each other."

"In my work, I'm not allowed to give help. I can only accept it."

"That makes it nice," she said.

"Does it?"

"For you."

We were silent for a little while.

"*Are* you working on the Endicott case, Donald?"

"No comment."

"I could help you."

"Many comments, but quite inaudible."

She swept her long, dark lashes down on her cheeks, held her eyes closed for half a second so that the darkness of the eyelashes showed against the smooth skin of her cheeks. Then she slowly raised her eyes to mine. She said suddenly, "All right, Donald. Here are the cards face up on the table. I'm twenty-three. I've been married. I'm a hell of a business woman. Aunt Martha died and left me the works. Most of it was property in Citrus Grove. I was an artist, not a real good one, just fair, advertising illustrations, things like that.

"A factory wants to come to Citrus Grove. I have the land the factory wants. At one time the land was residential property. I need to get a zoning ordinance changed. Any other city would change the ordinance just as a matter of course. Citrus Grove doesn't do things that way."

"How does Citrus Grove do things?" I asked.

"Citrus Grove," she said, "is under the dominance of the mayor."

"And who is the mayor?"

"Charles Franklin Taber. They had a reasonably honest government. They had a chief of police who was on the square. Taber made speeches. He gave interviews to the Press.

"Somebody's behind Taber. I don't know who it is, but there are too many brains being used to have everything originate with that lunk of a Taber.

"Anyway a fairly competent mayor was defeated at the polls. Charles Franklin Taber was swept in on what he called a 'wave of reform'. He found an officer who was taking something on the side, and made it look like the whole police force was corrupt. The honest chief of police was fired. A new chief of police was imported so that he would be 'free of local politics and free from local pressures.' That was put in quotes."

"Drude Nickerson?" I asked.

"Drude Nickerson *was* a cab-driver. He is a cousin of the mayor. *Now* Drude Nickerson goes in for bigger things. Drude Nickerson came to call on me. Nickerson knew about a lot of things. He knew all about the secret negotiations for the factory. He knew all about the property I had inherited.

"I told Drude Nickerson about how much good the factory would do the city, about the payroll it would bring in, and the people who would come, the increase in building and all of that."

"And what did Nickerson say?" I asked.

"Nickerson laughed. Nickerson told me not to be naïve. He told me that if I waited for the zoning ordinance to be changed I would wait a long, long time. He said business wasn't being done on that kind of a basis."

"On what kind of a basis was it being done?"

"On a cash basis."

"You donated?"

"Eventually, yes."

"How much?"

"Fifteen thousand, three payments of five thousand each."

I whistled.

"Was I a sucker, Donald?"

"Was the zoning ordinance changed?"

"Not yet. I only gave him the money two weeks ago. He said he would keep about a thousand for himself, that the rest of it had to be handled to build up political pressures, lobbying and things of that sort."

"And then?"

"Then he went and got himself killed in a traffic accident."

"And what was your interest in the body?"

"Not in the body. In the clothes the body was wearing at the time of the accident. He told me that he wouldn't actually let go of the money until he was assured the ordinance would pass and that to protect me in case anything should happen to him he'd have the cash in a safe-deposit box and the key to that box and a note saying the money was my property would be in his wallet."

"You believed that?"

"I did at the time."

"*Was* the note in his wallet?"

"I don't know. They gave me a regular bum's rush out of Susanville. They said I'd have to take up my claim with the adminstrator of the estate."

"You didn't see his wallet?"

"They didn't even let me get to first base.

"Now then, Donald, I've put my cards on the table. I've tried to play it smart. I've tried to outwit you. I've tried to be seductive. I've tried to ... shucks, I don't know, I guess I've been doing business with crooks for so long I thought everyone was crooked. You're square, and you ... you're decent."

"I can't help you," I told her.

"Why?"

"Because I'm working on something else for someone else. I can get information, but I can't give it out. I'll tell you one thing."

"What?"

"Don't shed any tears over Drude Nickerson's unfortunate demise."

"Tears for that crook!" she blazed. "What I want to know is what's going to happen to the zoning ordinance? I wouldn't cry over that two-timing——"

"Wait a moment, I guess I'm not supposed to speak ill of the dead. It isn't supposed to be the sporting thing to do."

"Go ahead and speak ill of him."

"What do you mean?"

"He isn't dead," I told her.

She looked at me with big eyes. "How do you know?"

"I don't know. I'm guessing," I said. "I don't think he's dead. I think the whole thing is a plant."

She sat very still for several minutes, thinking things over. Suddenly she looked up at me and said, "Donald, you're a darling and you may kiss me good night. What's more it's not going to be a cold, chaste kiss. Get ready, Donald, for an experience. You're about to receive an osculatory award from a grateful woman."

It was everything she said it was going to be.

CHAPTER SEVEN

I CAUGHT the six o'clock plane for Los Angeles and got to the office about the time Bertha Cool did.

"Get my wire?" I asked.

"Get your wire!" Bertha Cool said. "Of course I got your wire. How drunk were you when you sent it?"

"Cold sober."

"What the hell did you think you were doing, going out in the desert to collect flora and fauna? You couldn't get excited over a commonplace plant. What the hell were you talking about?"

"Didn't you understand what I meant?" I asked. "I wanted you to warn our client. The thing was a plant."

"What was?"

"Drude Nickerson's death."

Bertha Cool blinked her sharp little eyes at me. "Why the hell didn't you say so?"

"I did. I sent you a wire."

Bertha did some thinking for a minute. "If that's a plant," she said, "our client could be in one hell of a mess."

"How come?"

Bertha said, "I was burning up the long-distance telephone wires trying to get in touch with you. I called every motel, hotel, rooming house and honky-tonk in Susanville."

"What's the matter?" I asked.

"We're fired. We don't have any more case."

"What's happened to the case?"

"The client got his information out of a newspaper and it was all the information he needed."

"What newspaper?" I asked.

"The *Citrus Grove Clarion*."

"What did that paper have to say?"

"The paper found out about the death of Drude Nickerson. It published quite a story about it, and said that with the death of Nickerson the last chance of ever solving the murder of Karl Carver Endicott had passed. The newspaper went on to comment that Nickerson was the only man who had seen the killer and who could have made an identification."

"And that interested our client?" I asked.

"Very much."

"What did he do?"

"Told me that he had all the information that he wanted, that it had been a pleasure to do business with us, that he felt certain we could have handled the matter in such a way that it

37

would have given him the greatest satisfaction, but there was no longer any need for us to concern ourselves. The matter was all taken care of. He had the information he wanted."

"How nice!" I said. "The widow of Karl Carver Endicott. What about her?"

"What do you mean, what about her?"

"Where is she?"

"What's that to us?"

"Let's find out," I said. I picked up the phone and told the office operator to put in a call for Elizabeth Endicott at Citrus Grove; that it was a person-to-person call, we'd talk with no one else if she wasn't there; that if she wasn't there, to find out where we could reach her. If she was at a telephone any place in the United States, we'd talk with her there.

Bertha was blinking her eyes at me as I hung up. "Are you nuts?" she asked.

"No."

"Those calls cost money."

"We still have expense money."

"Not now we don't. The case is over."

"For your information," I said, "if the thing is happening the way I have it doped out, the case is just starting. Whether we'll be in it or not, I don't know."

Bertha said, "You must be off your rocker, Donald, or else you're thinking about some other case. Our client, John Dittmar Ansel, called up and told us there was no more case, to discontinue expenses, to make an accounting. Do you understand?"

"Sure I understand. Ansel is the one who doesn't understand."

"What doesn't he understand?"

"That's he walking into a trap."

The phone rang and the girl at the office exchange stated that Mrs. Endicott was away and would be gone for about a week, that there was no place where she could be reached.

I relayed the information to Bertha.

"Well?" Bertha asked.

I said. "I suppose we *could* telephone our correspondents in Las Vegas, Nevada, and Yuma, Arizona, and have them on the job so we could tip Ansel off. But that's going to cost a lot of money and I don't think he'd pay to have his wedding interrupted."

"Could you blame him?" Bertha asked.

"No," I said, and started for the door.

"Now wait a minute! Don't walk out of here without telling me what this is all about," Bertha snapped.

"I don't know yet, not for sure."

"When will you know?"

"When they arrest John Dittmar Ansel and Elizabeth Endicott just as they step up to the altar prepared to enter into the holy bonds of wedlock."

"Are you kidding?"

"No."

"Well then, who the devil *is* our client, John Dittmar Ansel?" she asked.

"For your information," I said, "John Dittmar Ansel is the man who was taken to Karl Carver Endicott's house in Drude Nickerson's taxicab on the fateful murder date."

Bertha thought that over a long time. "Can they prove it?"

"Of course they can prove it. Otherwise, they wouldn't have gone to all this trouble to get him to come out into the open and furnish them with proof of motivation."

"Fry me for an oyster!" Bertha said, as I walked out and left her sitting there, snapping her fingers in an ecstasy of exasperation.

CHAPTER EIGHT

I WOKE up about one-thirty and had trouble getting back to sleep. A whole series of events were chasing around in my mind trying to fit themselves into a pattern.

Three or four times I would doze off, only to waken with a start as all of the various ideas started chasing each other around like puppies at play. Finally about two-thirty I slipped into fitful sleep. It was broken by dreams and finally shattered by the ringing of the telephone bell.

I groped for the receiver.

Bertha Cool was on the line. I knew by the tone of her voice that we'd struck pay dirt.

"Donald," she said in her most cooing voice, but mouthing the words as though each one had been a dollar rung up in the cash register, "Bertha hates to bother you at night, but *could* you get dressed and hurry to the office?"

"What's the matter?" I asked.

"I can't explain, Donald, but we have a client who is in very great trouble. We——"

I said, "Listen, Bertha, are you dealing with the man who was arrested, with the woman who was with him, or with some lawyer."

"The second," she said.

"I'll be right up. Where are you now?"

"I'm at the office, Donald. It's the strangest, the weirdest story you ever heard in your life."

"Mrs. Endicott there with you?"

"Yes," Bertha said shortly.

"I'll be up."

I tumbled out of bed, into a shower, hit the high spots with an electric razor, jumped into clothes and drove through deserted streets to the office building.

The night janitor was accustomed to the crazy goings-on of a detective agency. He grumbled a bit about people who tried to run offices on a twenty-four-hour basis, but took me up.

I latch-keyed the door and went on into Bertha's private office.

Bertha was being very maternal to a sad-eyed woman around thirty, who was sitting perfectly still in the chair, but who had been twisting her gloves until they looked like a piece of rope.

Bertha beamed. "This is Mrs. Endicott, Donald."

"How do you do, Mrs. Endicott," I said.

She gave me a cold hand and a warm smile.

"Donald," Bertha said, "this is the damnedest story you ever heard in your life. This is absolutely out of this world. This is—— Well, I want Mrs. Endicott to tell you in her own words."

Mrs. Endicott was a brunette. She had big dark eyes, high cheekbones, smooth complexion, and, aside from a general air of funereal sadness about her, might have been a professional poker player. She'd learned somewhere to keep her emotions under complete control. Her face was as expressionless as the marble slab of a gravestone.

"Do you mind, dear?" Bertha said.

"Not at all," Mrs. Endicott said in a low but strong voice. "After all, that's why we got Mr. Lam up out of bed, and he can't very well work on a case unless he knows the facts."

"If you can just give him the highlights," Bertha said, "I can fill him in later on."

"Very well," Mrs. Endicott said and twisted her gloves so tight it seemed the stitching would start ripping.

"This goes back almost seven years," she said.

I nodded as she paused.

"Just the highspots," Bertha said, in a voice that was dripping with synthetic sympathy.

"John Ansel and I were in love. We were going to get married. John was working for Karl Carver Endicott.

"Karl sent John Ansel to Brazil. After John got to Brazil, Karl sent him on an expedition up the Amazon. It was a suicide trip. Karl claimed he was looking for oil prospects. There were two men in the party. He offered each of them a twenty-thousand dollar bonus to make the trip *if* they completed the mission successfully.

"They were, of course, under no obligations to go, but John wanted that money very badly because that would have enabled us to get married and he could have started a business of his own. That trip was legalized murder. It was carefully designed to be such. I didn't know it at the time. The expedition didn't stand one chance in a thousand. The cards were stacked against them, and Karl Carver Endicott made damn certain that the cards *were* stacked against them.

"After a while Karl came to me with tears in his eyes. He said he had just received word that the entire party had been wiped out. They were, he said, long overdue and he had sent planes out to search. He'd also sent out ground parties. He'd spared no expense.

"It was a terrific shock to me. Karl did his best to comfort me and finally offered me security and an opportunity to patch up my life."

She stopped talking for a moment and gave her gloves such a vicious twist that the skin over the knuckles went white.

"You married him?" I asked.

"I married him."

"And then?"

"Later on he fired one of his secretaries. She was the first who told me. I couldn't believe my ears. But everything fitted in with other facts as I'd come to know them.

"This ex-secretary told me that Karl Endicott had made a very careful examination in order to pick out a locale for a suicide trip. He had sent John Ansel to his death just as surely as though he had stood him up in front of a firing squad."

"Did you go to your husband and face him with the facts?" I asked.

"There wasn't time," she said. "I had the most terrible, the most awful, unexpected, devastating experience. The telephone rang. I answered it. John Ansel was on the line. The other members of the expedition had perished. John had survived absolutely incredible hardships in the jungle, had finally reached civilization, and then had learned that I was married."

"What did you do?"

She said, "In those days I hadn't learned to control my emotions. I became completely, utterly hysterical. I told John that I belonged to him, that I always had belonged to him, that I had been tricked into marriage. I told John I must see him. I told him that I was leaving Karl immediately.

"And then I did something that I shouldn't have done. Then I . . . I want you to understand, Mr. Lam, that I was hysterical. I . . . I was suffering from a terrific shock."

"What did you do?" I asked.

"I told John over the telephone exactly what the score was. I told him that he had been sent into the jungle on a mission that constituted legalized murder. I told him that Karl wanted him out of the way and that the whole thing had been deliberately planned so that he could trick me."

"Then what?" I asked.

She said, "For a while there was an absolute silence, then a click. I couldn't tell whether the person at the other end had hung up the telephone or whether the connexion had been broken. I finally got the operator and told her I'd been cut off. She said my party had hung up."

"What date was this?" I asked.

"That," she said bitterly, "was the date my husband met his death."

"Where was John Ansel when he phoned you?"

"In Los Angeles at the airport."

"All right. What happened?"

"I can't explain everything that happened without telling you something about Karl. Karl was ruthless, possessive, cold-blooded, and diabolically clever. When Karl wanted something, he wanted it. He wanted me. I think one of the main reasons he wanted me was because, after he had made the first overture, he found that I was not responsive.

"By the time of John's telephone call, things were getting to a point where I had learned a great deal about Karl's character, and I think he had gone a long way towards getting over his infatuation, if you want to call it that. After all, being married to an unwilling woman whose heart is elsewhere satisfied Karl's love of conquest, but that was about all."

"You faced your husband with what you had learned?"

"I did, Mr. Lam, and I would have given anything if I had only used my head instead of letting my emotions run away with me. However, for months I had been fighting myself, controlling my emotions, keeping myself under wraps. When I blew up, I blew up all over. We had a terrific scene."

"What did you do?"

"I slapped his face. I—if I had had a weapon I would have killed him."

"And then you walked out?"

"I walked out."

"And what happened?"

"John Ansel had been at the airport. There was a helicopter service to Citrus Grove. He took the helicopter, picked up a taxicab and drove directly to Karl's estate. I learned afterwards what happened."

"All right. What did happen?"

"John rang the doorbell. Karl answered the bell personally. Karl knew, of course, that John was alive because in my anger I had told him. John hadn't communicated with the office when he had reached civilization because of certain discoveries that he had encountered on the expedition. Still loyal to Karl's interests, he had been planning on making a confidential communication to Karl before disclosing that he had survived the jungle expedition and facing the inevitable newspaper inquiries. However, I think that even before I told him, Karl had learned somehow that John had returned."

"Go on."

"I think perhaps Karl had been intending to face it out. After all, John couldn't *prove* anything, or so Karl thought, but one look at John's face and Karl knew that John knew and ... Well, the John Dittmar Ansel who had been sent to Brazil on that suicide mission was not the John Dittmar Ansel who returned. John had lived in the jungle. He had lived with death at his elbow. He had been part of a constant struggle between life and death."

"Go on," I said.

"Karl took one look at John and was shaken. He led the way to an upstairs office. He told John that he would be with him in a moment and stepped into an adjoining room.

"You have met John, Mr. Lam. I think you're a good judge of character. There is something psychic about John. He is essentially a gentle soul, but as I say, he had lived in the jungle. He had been through unspeakable hardships, but he had always retained that sensitive, artistic insight.

"John has told me that after a few seconds he knew what Karl had in mind. Karl intended to murder him. He intended to shoot him down and claim that he had shot in self-defence. He intended to work some scheme of planting a revolver by John's body and perhaps firing a shot from that revolver. He would claim that John had accused him of stealing his sweetheart, of——"

"Never mind the window dressing," I said. "Just what did John do?"

"John quietly left the room and tiptoed down the stairs. He decided that he would face Karl in court and that he would face him with witnesses so that he would never again give Karl an opportunity to shoot and claim that he was acting in self-defence."

"And what happened?"

"John had just opened the front door and was leaving the house when he heard the revolver shot."

"John knew that you had left?" I asked.

"He did. That was another of his telepathic or psychic hunches, or whatever you want to call them. He said that the minute he entered the house he knew that I had left. Perhaps it was something in the expression on Karl's face. Perhaps it was just a feeling."

"It wasn't anything that Karl had said?" I asked.

"No. He says not."

"All right, what did John do?"

"He walked out to the highway. He hitch-hiked back to Los Angeles. He read in the papers of Karl's death, and read about the taxi driver who described him so perfectly that John knew that if anyone knew he was alive he would be accused of Karl's murder and he wouldn't stand a ghost of a chance.

"John had every reason in the world to kill Karl, but he ... Well, you can see for yourself, Mr. Lam, unless the real murderer of Karl could be found, John didn't stand a whisper of a chance."

"So what happened?"

She said, "I knew where John would be. I went to him that night. We discussed matters. It was decided that John would have to keep out of sight until the person who had killed Karl could be brought to justice. That would be easy because everyone thought John was dead. So we started a long nightmare.

"John kept under cover. I did everything I could to solve the murder of my husband. I had to go back and take charge of the estate. I inherited Karl's money because he hadn't had time to disinherit me and I never enjoyed anything more than stepping into the fortune Karl had left."

"But how about the person who murdered Karl Endicott?"

"Cooper Hale murdered Karl Endicott," she said, "but we can't prove it. We're never going to be able to prove it. Cooper Hale is too smart. Hale knew in some way what was taking place. He followed Karl when Karl went upstairs. Remember Karl was getting out a revolver which he intended to plant on John's body. Karl intended to call Hale in as a witness to show that the shooting had been in self-defence.

"Hale stepped into the room, calmly picked up the revolver, shot Karl through the head, then went back downstairs and telephoned for the police."

"What was Hale's motivation?" I asked.

"That I don't know. I do know this: that my husband had withdrawn twenty thousand dollars from the bank that day. I think he knew John was alive and was preparing to pay him the twenty thousand bonus which had been agreed upon. For some reason he wanted to pay that in cash. That twenty thousand vanished.

"However, for two months my husband had been paying blackmail, ten thousand a month.

"Hale had been a clerk. Suddenly he became affluent. Hale has grown steadily during the years since Karl's death. He is now an influential banker."

"All right. Let's get down to the present," I said. "What happened?"

"Police watched me day and night. They sensed that I might be in communication with the person they felt was the murderer. I was very, very careful. I went into hibernation in order to protect John. Gradually the police relaxed their vigil. It became possible for John and me to see each other, but we had to meet at rare intervals and under such surreptitious circumstances that it was heartbreaking. Remember everyone thought John Ansel was dead.

"Drude Nickerson was, of course, the only witness. And then I read that Drude Nickerson had been killed in a traffic accident. I didn't dare to show interest in the matter, but we felt that it would be possible for John to contact a detective agency, provided the detective agency knew nothing about where John was living so that if anything happened the police couldn't follow up and arrest John.

"Then we found out that Nickerson definitely was dead and that the police had thrown up their hands in the case. I suppose we were terribly foolish but we had been starving ourselves emotionally over the years, we had been meeting so surreptitiously that much of the pleasure was taken from the meetings, and we had reason to believe that the police had virtually written the case off the books.

"The very thought of being able to live together openly as man and wife, of being able to face the world, completely swept us off our feet. We decided that sooner or later we were going to have to face the whole situation, and we decided to face it now."

"So," I said, "you walked into the trap."

She twisted her gloves violently. "We walked into the trap. We flew to Yuma. We walked into a justice of the peace to get married, and the officers were waiting. Oh, it was so terribly cruel! Why did they have to strike at that time? At least they could have held off until we were married, and——"

"And then they couldn't have forced you to testify," I said. "They let the thing go right up to the time of the wedding so they could prove motivation."

"It was all a trap," she admitted. "The police had arranged the thing as an elaborate plant. They knew that Drude Nickerson was their only witness. They knew that if he died they didn't have a case. So they—well, they prepared this elaborate trap. They fixed it up with Nickerson. Tomorrow the newspapers will state that the reports of his death were erroneous, that they were based on the identification of some hitchhiker who happened to have one of Nickerson's cards in his pocket."

I shook my head. "No, they won't."

"What do you mean, they won't?" she said. "They've already told us that——"

"They'll have another idea by the time they think things over," I said. "They will ballyhoo it for what it was, a clever police trap by which they lured a fugitive from justice, who had eluded them for six years, into the police net."

She twisted her gloves again, and this time her face twisted with feeling, but she was dry-eyed and her voice was as low-pitched and as deadly as the sound made by a snake's rattles.

"I could kill the man who did this to us."

"That won't help," I said.

"What am I going to do?" she asked.

That was Bertha's cue. "Mrs. Endicott has placed herself entirely in our hands, Donald, and there's no need at all to worry about the financial arrangements. We have worked those out. She got in touch with me just as soon as the officers made the arrest.

"Now, Donald, we want you to get busy and work on this case. There's enough involved so we can completely exclude all other business matters from our minds and concentrate on this case."

I took the telephone directory from Bertha's desk.

"The first thing you want is a lawyer," I said, "and you want him fast."

She said, "I have already thought of that. There are two outstanding lawyers in Los Angeles whose names command respect. I'll——"

"Forget it!" I told her. "The case is going to be tried in Orange County. You want someone in Santa Ana. You also want someone who will listen to reason."

"What do you mean, listen to reason?" she asked.

"Listen to me," I said and reached for the telephone, dialled long distance and said, "Operator, this is an emergency call. I want to talk with Bernard Quinn, a lawyer at Santa Ana, California. His residence number is Sycamore 3-9865. Just start ringing and keep ringing until you get an answer."

CHAPTER NINE

It was just breaking daylight as we parked our cars in the deserted street in front of the building where Barney Quinn had his offices.

Quinn was waiting for us.

He was a stockily built chap who had had a reasonable amount of experience. He had been in law school with me.

We explained the circumstances to him. He was, of course, familiar with all of the general facts concerning the murder of Karl Carver Endicott. It had been a big murder mystery in its day and the local papers had played it up for all it was worth.

"They didn't try to hold you?" he asked Mrs. Endicott.

She shook her head.

"They'll come back after you as a material witness," he said. "The district attorney will be very fatherly and very nice. He will explain that undoubtedly you were taken in, that if you'll make a complete statement to him there won't be any trouble, but he's going to have to call you as a witness and all of that sort of stuff."

"What do I do?" she asked her lips clamped in a thin line of angry determination.

"Tell him to go to hell," Quinn said. "Not in those words of course, but in words having that same general meaning, only more advantageous to the defence. Tell him that he simply doesn't know John Dittmar Ansel, that there has been a horrible mistake, that Ansel wouldn't hurt a fly, that you have never been satisfied with the investigative work that was done in the case, that your husband's murderer is reading the newspapers right now and laughing at the manner in which the police are busily engaged in trying to work up a case against the wrong man.

"Make it dramatic! Pour it on! Let the words come spouting forth with feeling! Put on an act. Then take refuge in tears and refuse to make any further statements. You have said all there is to say, and that's all you're going to say.

"When they ask you if you refuse to be of any help in the case, if you refuse to co-operate, become indignant and tell them, 'Certainly not!' that you will give them all the co-operation they want, that you will make all the statements they want, but from that point on your statements are to be made in the office of Bernard Quinn who is attorney for John D. Ansel.

"Think you can do that?"

"Of course I can do it."

"And you will?"

"You can count on me."

"All right," Quinn said. "Now I'm going to try and see Ansel. Do you know if he waived extradition, Mrs. Endicott?"

"I don't know a thing about what happened. They took him into custody. I tried to talk with him and they wouldn't let me. It was in the wedding chapel. They rushed him out and loaded him into a car and went away from there as though they were going to a fire. They evidently had men covering both Las Vegas and Yuma. The minute we took out a licence we were marked for the slaughter."

Quinn said, "If they didn't get him to waive extradition, we'll fight extradition. We'll fight all along the way. If he did waive extradition, I'll get in touch with him just as soon as they book him here in the county jail."

Quinn turned to me. "Lam," he said, "you've been of inestimable help on a couple of cases I've handled. We want your co-operation in this."

"You're going to have it," Bertha Cool said.

Quinn said to Mrs. Endicott, "It is essential that I have the right kind of assistance in getting the facts. I want you to make arrangements with these detectives to——"

"Arrangements have already been made," Bertha interrupted with firm finality. "You don't need to go into that, Mr. Quinn. You can count on our co-operation and assistance."

Quinn thought that over, looked into Bertha Cool's cold, pale eyes, pursed his lips, played with a pencil for a minute, then said to Mrs. Endicott, "I'm going to want a retainer."

"How much?" she asked.

"This isn't going to be a cheap case."

"I didn't ask you to make it a cheap case."

"Twenty thousand dollars," he said.

She opened her purse and took out a cheque book.

"The man who is responsible for all this," she said, "is Cooper Hale."

Quinn held up his hand. "Don't mention any names. All that you know is that John Ansel is innocent. You leave the rest to me."

"Very well," she said.

Quinn looked at me. "And I'll depend on you folks to get the facts."

Whenever a client was making out a cheque Bertha considered the moment sacred. The slightest sound, the intrusion of a comment might be an interruption.

Bertha sat there, holding her breath, while Mrs. Endicott's

pen moved over the tinted oblong of paper. When the cheque had been signed, Bertha let out the breath she had been holding during the operation. She watched the passage of the cheque from Mrs. Endicott's hand to Barney Quinn's hand. Then she inhaled a deep breath.

"When do we eat?" she asked.

CHAPTER TEN

THE morning newspapers had headlines: "MURDER SUS-PECT ENTERS POLICE TRAP."

There was quite a story. The six-year-old murder mystery of Karl Carver Endicott, a multi-millionaire, who had extensive oil interests throughout the country as well as substantial acreage in citrus lands, and had been mysteriously slain in his home, was on the point of being solved, according to police.

Police had long had a good description of the killer. A man who at that time was driving a taxicab, but who had since become prosperous through real estate and other investments, had furnished a most detailed description of the last man who had seen Endicott alive.

Police had long acted on the theory that the killer, whoever he might have been, had been actuated by romantic motives. They also knew that the fatal weakness of their case was that Drude Nickerson, the former taxi driver, was the only person who could furnish eyewitness identification.

Therefore, as a last desperate resort, police baited a trap with the co-operation of the Press.

When an unidentified hitch-hiker had been killed near Susanville, police had arranged for Drude Nickerson to keep out of circulation for a few days. They had made a tentative identification of the body of the traffic victim as that of Drude Nickerson and, thanks to co-operation on the part of the Press, had lulled the suspect into a false sense of security.

Having kept under cover for years, John Dittmar Ansel, who was himself supposed to have perished in the Amazon years before, had come into the open. Almost within a matter of hours of the announcement that police were closing their files in the Endicott murder case because of the death of the only witness who could make an identification, John Dittmar Ansel and Elizabeth Endicott, the wealthy widow of Karl Carver Endicott, had appeared in Yuma, Arizona, had taken out a marriage licence and were on the point of becoming man and wife when police, who had been waiting in the wings, so to speak, had swooped down upon the pair, whisking Ansel off to jail.

No charges had as yet been made against Elizabeth Endicott, but the district attorney of Orange County announced that he wanted to question her as a material witness and intended to do so. His questioning, he indicated, would seek to determine whether Mrs Endicott had known that Ansel was alive and where he had been concealing himself during the past six years, the number of times Mrs. Endicott had seen Ansel, what steps if

51

any she had taken to assist in his concealment, and whether she knew anything concerning the murder of her husband which had not previously been disclosed to authorities.

The newspaper pointed out that it was to be remembered Mrs. Endicott had left the house shortly before the murder. The time of the murder had been accurately fixed and Mrs. Endicott had an alibi of sorts in that apparently she had been purchasing gasoline for her automobile at a point some two miles from the house at the exact time the murder had been committed.

The district attorney stated, however, that a new and searching inquiry into this time element was going to be launched, that the entire case was going to be given a thorough and exhaustive investigation.

We had breakfast and drove back to Los Angeles. I went to a barber shop, had a shave, a massage and a lot of hot towels.

When I reached the office, Elsie Brand, my secretary, handed me a note with a number I was to call.

"Any name?" I asked.

"No name, just a seductive voice. She said she had met you in Reno, and would you care to call?"

I called.

Stella Karis said, "I wondered if you'd like to have breakfast with me?"

"I'm a working man," I told her. "I had breakfast a long time ago?"

"How long?"

"Hours."

"Then you could have a second breakfast."

"Where are you?"

"In my apartment."

"How did you get back?" I asked.

"I drove."

"When did you get in?"

"About eleven o'clock last night."

"Read the papers?"

"No."

"Some news in connexion with Citrus Grove," I said. "You might like to take a look."

"I'll read them. The point is, do you come for breakfast?"

"When?"

"Now."

"Where?"

"The Monaster Apartments."

"I'll be up," I told her.

Elsie Brand, who had been listening to the conversation, had a poker face. "Do you want to dictate this correspondence now, Donald?" she asked.

"Not now," I said. "I'm busy."

"So I gathered."

"Now look, Elsie, if Bertha wants me, I've been in and now I've gone out again. You don't know where. You know Bertha well enough so you can tell whether it's something important or whether she's just checking up.

"If it's something really important, call me at this number, but don't let anyone have that number, and don't call unless it's something really important. Understand?"

She nodded.

"Good girl," I told her and patted her shoulder as I went out.

The Monaster apartment house was a swank little place and Stella Karis had a nice apartment with sunlight pouring in through eastern windows.

She had on some sort of fluffy creation which kept popping open around the throat, and long bell-shaped sleeves that would have trailed in the coffee, across the fried eggs and into the toast if she hadn't been some kind of an indoor acrobat and managed to grab the trailing cloth just in time.

I watched her with fascination.

It was a nice breakfast. I didn't particularly need it, but it tasted good.

"Donald," she said after I had cleaned up my plate. "You know something?"

"What?"

"I told you about this Nickerson."

"Uh-huh."

"He isn't dead."

"I told you to read the papers."

"I didn't need to. He called me at seven o'clock this morning."

"Surprised to hear his voice?"

"I was terribly shocked. I—well, I had hoped I wasn't going to have anything more to do with him."

"You hate to come out and say you hoped he was dead, don't you?"

"All right, I hoped he was dead."

"That's better."

"He called and told me that he needed ten thousand dollars more. He said that the members of the city council had been a little more obstinate than he had expected, that there were five of them and it was going to take five thousand apiece. He said at that price it wouldn't leave a cent for him, that he was embarrassed because he hadn't been able to deliver the goods as promised, so he'd simply act as middle-man and go-between. He said he'd make me a present of his services and he wouldn't take a cent."

"Philanthropist, eh?" I asked.

"That's what he said."

"What did you do?"

"I told him I'd have to think it over."

I grinned. "So then you cooked breakfast and baited me over here?"

She waited for a moment, then smiled and said, "All right, then I cooked breakfast and baited you over here."

"I'm a professional man," I said. "I have a partner. We have to sell our services."

"I'm willing to buy your services."

"I can't sell them in this case. I can't have you for a client."

"Why not?"

"There might be a conflict in interests."

"And I can't become your client—no matter *what* I pay?"

"Not in regard to Nickerson."

"As a friend, could you make a suggestion?"

"As a friend, yes."

"What?"

"Tell him to go to hell," I said. "Tell him you want your fifteen grand back."

"That I want money *back* from a man like Nickerson?" she asked. "Are you crazy?"

"I'm not telling you you're going to get anything back," I said. "Tell him you *want* your money back."

"Then what?"

"Then he'll ask you what you're going to do."

"Then what?"

"Tell him that you have plans that will rip Citrus Grove wide open."

"Then what do I do?"

"Hang up."

"Then what happens?"

"The zoning ordinance gets passed and you can complete the deal with your factory."

"You're sure?"

"Hell, no, I'm not sure. It depends on how deeply the council members are mixed into this thing. It depends on how much Nickerson has been pulling your leg. It depends on whether he's even given a dime of the fifteen grand to anyone else."

"Of course," she said, "I don't have a thing on him."

"You paid the fifteen thousand in cash?"

"Yes."

"How?"

"In three instalments of five thousand each."

"Where did you get the money?"

"From the bank, of course."

"How?"

"I drew out cheques payable to cash."

"Five grand at a time?"

"That's right."

"Why the three instalments?"

"That's the way Nickerson wanted it."

"How long an interval between the three instalments?"

"One day each. He wanted five thousand on a Monday, five thousand on a Tuesday, and five thousand on a Wednesday."

"Where did you pay him the money?"

"Here."

"In this apartment?"

"Yes."

I said, "Tell me about this factory."

She hesitated.

"Or don't. Just as you see fit," I told her. "And don't tell me anything in confidence. I'm working on another matter. As long as it becomes advisable to play your case as a trump card in this case I'll do it."

"You mean the Endicott murder case?"

"I could mean that."

"After all I don't know but what I've kept some things to myself that I should have publicized."

I looked at my watch.

"All right, I'm going to tell you," she said.

"The factory is a novelty company. It wants to make citrus candies out of some sort of gumdrop material, oranges that look like the real thing only on a miniature scale, shipped in little packing boxes. Lemons, the same way. It wants to make a lot of Southern California souvenirs, catering to the gift trade and stuff that can be sent back East. Souvenirs from California. It wants the Citrus Grove address on its stationery and printed on the boxes. The management feels that the words 'Citrus Grove, California' will be a good trademark."

"They're going at it on a big scale?"

"On a big scale. They're going to sell direct by mail. They're going to place their products all around at various places where people buy gifts. At the airports, in railroad stations, at scenic points."

"How much land do they want?"

"Ten acres."

"Ten acres!"

"That's right."

"What in the world do they want with ten acres?"

"Because this plot of ten acres has facilities for a railroad siding, and——"

"A railroad siding!"

She nodded.

I thought things over. "Are you dealing direct with the company, or with a real estate broker of some sort?"

"I'm dealing direct with the company. The president of the company is a man by the name of Seward, Jed C. Seward."

I gave the matter a lot of thought. "Look," I said. "All of this ten acres isn't zoned."

"Part of it is zoned as residential property. Part of it is in a limited business district."

"How come there are ten acres without buildings that——"

"Oh, there are buildings on it," she said. "The buildings are little, cheap cracker-box affairs."

"How come you own them all then? How does it happen that the ownership isn't scattered around?"

"Because my aunt was shrewd. She said this piece of property would be exceedingly valuable as the town grew, and she worked very quietly over a period of years buying up pieces of property as they came on the market. Then finally she went in with a whirlwind finish and paid some very, very fancy prices for some of the holdouts."

"And now you have it all?"

She nodded. "I was the only relative. I've got property I don't know what to do with. I don't like managing property. I'm an artist. I like to draw and paint. Now I'm stinking rich."

She looked at me speculatively. "I need a manager, some shrewd man who can understand me——"

"Want some advice?" I interrupted.

"From you, yes."

"Go to your bank," I said. "Turn everything over to their trust department. Tell them you want income and let them turn your holdings into blue chip securities and pay you the income."

"I wouldn't like that. Banks are too impersonal. It would be like declaring myself incompetent and having the bank as a guardian."

"You'll need a guardian if you start looking around for congenial property managers."

"I can trust my instincts."

"That's proof you need a guardian."

"I know what I'm doing."

"All right. Skip it. When's Nickerson going to get in touch with you?"

"Sometime this afternoon."

"Tell him to go to hell," I said.

"Donald, it's a nice deal. The ... Well, if I could get that ordinance through, I could——"

I shook my head.

"Why not?"

"You won't get it through."

"Why not?"

"Because you're a babe in the woods," I told her. "A novelty company doesn't want ten acres with railroad siding facilities."

"But they do! They've put up a big cash deposit."

"And," I went on, "Nickerson is playing things smart. The fifteen grand was just the entering wedge."

"But I've got so much invested now that I——"

"That's the way Nickerson's figures," I said. "And after you've put in twenty-five, you'll have that much more invested. Then you'll have to put in another twenty. And after you've got that much in, you can't afford to back out. You'll take him into partnership."

"But Donald, it . . . it means so much and it seems so foolish to——"

"Look," I said, "you're dealing with a crooked city government. You're dealing with a crooked guy. He has now become the main witness in a murder case. He's going to get ripped apart when he gets on the witness stand. Get out from under. Tell him to go to hell. You asked my advice, and you've got it. It may or may not be worth much, but it's at least worth two fried eggs and a cup of coffee."

Her face coloured. "I wasn't trying to . . . Well, it's not that way. I wanted to make you an offer. I like you. I need someone to——"

"Forget it!" I told her. "Go to your bank. Do what I said."

She got mad. "You think my instincts aren't to be trusted, don't you? You think I'd pick someone who was dishonest. Are *you* dishonest? I give you a chance to rook me and do you take it? Not you! You tell me to go to a bank, and then you say I can't pick men who——"

The phone rang and kept on ringing. She gave an exclamation of disgust, picked up the receiver, said, "Hello," and then frowned.

"It's for you, Donald," she said.

I took the telephone.

Elsie Brand's voice said, "The case has blown wide open, Donald. Barney Quinn has made some sort of an announcement from Santa Ana. We're in the case up to our necks, and Bertha Cool is having hysterics. A couple of newspaper reporters are in the office."

"Hold them there. I'll be right over," I said.

"What do you mean, *right* over?" she asked sceptically.

"I mean *right* over."

I grabbed my hat, "Thanks for the breakfast, sweetheart," and made a bolt for the door.

CHAPTER ELEVEN

BERTHA COOL'S eyes lit up as I entered the office. The newspapermen had been giving her a bad time.

There were two reporters and a photographer. I shook hands all around.

"What do you want to know, boys?" I asked.

They were top-flight men and they didn't beat around the bush. "You're working for the defendants in this Endicott case?"

"Are there two?" I asked.

"They may be."

"We're working for Barney Quinn," I said.

"How did they happen to pick Barney Quinn as their lawyer?"

"Isn't he a good lawyer?"

"I don't know. I'm wondering how they happened to pick him."

"You'd better ask Ansel about that."

"Look, Lam. You've been working on this thing for several days. You went down to Citrus Grove, started prowling around in the newspaper files. You asked questions about Endicott."

"That's right," I said.

Bertha gave a little gasp. "I denied it, Donald," she said.

I sat on the edge of the desk and grinned. "Don't lie to the newspapers, Bertha. It's bad business. Tell them the truth or keep quiet."

"Then it's the truth? You were down working on this Endicott case?"

"That isn't what I said."

"What did you say?"

"I was down in Citrus Grove working. I consulted the back files of the *Citrus Grove Clarion*. I asked about Endicott."

"Isn't that the same thing?"

"That's not the same thing."

"Why?"

"Because I was looking up something that wasn't connected with the murder. I didn't know Endicott had been murdered until after I got in conversation with the people at the newspaper office."

"Phooey!"

"That's right, boys. I'm giving it to you on the square."

"What did you go down there on?"

"Another matter."

"What was it?"

58

I said, "I was looking up certain matters for a client whose name I can't disclose. For your information, Citrus Grove is about to become the centre of one of the biggest industrial developments in this part of the country. A large eastern auto-motive manufacturer is looking for the proper place for a western assembly plant with adequate space, railroad facilities, a sufficient opportunity for residential expansion and all that goes with it.

"Citrus Grove has been tentatively selected as the spot. In order to get the spot the company wants, it became necessary to change the zoning restrictions on a piece of property adjoining holdings the company had secretly acquired. In the interests of community expansion, in the interests of adding to the in-dustrial life of Southern California, the zoning ordinance should have been changed as a matter of course. Actually there has been a delay and the company has been concerned about that delay. There were indications that certain influential per-sons were trying to get a handout. The company wanted that situation investigated. Actually the company doesn't want to invest in a city where there is corruption."

"We can quote you on that?" the reporters asked.

"You may quote me."

"On this plant coming to Southern California?"

"That's right."

"What plant?"

"I can't divulge that information."

"You said it's an eastern automobile manufacturer?"

"I have said that," I told them, "and you can quote me but don't be too surprised if it should turn out to be an establish-ment of similar size in some other industry."

Pencils were making frantic notes over the notebooks. Bertha was looking at me with startled, incredulous surprise depicted all over her face.

"And what were you doing down in Citrus Grove looking through the back files of the newspaper?"

"I was trying to get some personal information about a character."

"Subsequently you went to Susanville?"

"Subsequently I went to Susanville."

"You encountered the Orange County sheriff up there and you were given the bum's rush out of town?"

"I was asked to leave town as a personal favour to someone on the police department down here."

"Why?"

"Because, as I understand it now, the police were baiting a trap for the person they thought was the murderer of Karl Carver Endicott. At the time I didn't know why. I was asked to withdraw as a personal favour and, because I convinced myself that the lead I was following was not going to be productive of anything, I withdrew."

"Is it safe to assume that the person you were investigating was in some way mixed in with the corruption you have mentioned?"

"It depends on what you mean by it being 'safe' to assume that. If you want to assume it, that's fine. If you want to publish that assumption, it *could* get you involved in a libel suit."

They thought that over. "How did you happen to get involved in this Endicott case?"

"Quinn retained us."

"When?"

"At an early hour this morning."

"Did he call you?"

"We discussed the matter over the phone, yes."

"Where did the conference take place?"

"In his office."

"Isn't it rather a coincidence that you should get in on two matters connected with Citrus Grove within the last few days?"

"That depends on what you mean. I think perhaps we should be grateful to the *Citrus Grove Clarion*. It published a story to the effect that I was investigating the Endicott murder case. That story was read by Barney Quinn. I wouldn't be too surprised if, under the circumstances, it had something to do with our employment in this Endicott case."

"What's Mrs. Endicott going to do? Is she going to cooperate with the authorities?"

"You'll have to ask Quinn about Mrs. Endicott."

"How did it happen that John Ansel, who was supposed to have been killed in the Amazon jungle several years ago, never let it be known that he was alive?"

"You'll have to ask Quinn about that."

"Why did he keep under cover?"

"I don't know. He may have been investigating something on his own. You'll have to ask Quinn."

"Is it true that Mrs. Endicott knew Ansel was alive before her husband was killed?"

I said, "Look, boys, you're wasting a lot of time. You've got a darn good story. Why don't you go out and put it in the papers? You know damn well we can't tell you anything about what any of the principals in the case are going to do. The only person who could make any announcement of that sort would be Barney Quinn.

"As it is, I've stuck my neck out. We're working on this Endicott case. You wanted a story. I've given you a brand new angle."

They exchanged glances and nodded. The photographer took

a picture of me sitting on the edge of Bertha's desk. He took a picture of Bertha and me "conferring". He took a picture of Bertha and me shaking hands.

They shook hands with us and left.

"You little bastard!" Bertha said. "They'll crucify you for that!"

"For what?"

"For all that cockeyed information."

"Wait and see," I told her.

CHAPTER TWELVE

THE story made headlines in the afternoon papers. The evening edition of the *Citrus Grove Clarion* contained a statement from Bailey Crosset, one of the city trustees of Citrus Grove.

Crosset denied unequivocally the slanderous accusation made by an "irresponsible Los Angeles detective" to the effect that any member or members of the city council of Citrus Grove had had their hands out or were standing in the path of progress.

There had, he admitted, been some off-the-record discussion concerning changing of a zoning ordinance in connexion with a tract of land. The city council had the matter under informal advisement.

Crosset stated that he had at no time received any money or ever expected to receive any money for any matter in connexion with his duties as city councilman. He was, however, in politics, and as a politician he was entitled to accept campaign contributions. He had accepted a campaign contribution from Drude Nickerson. The amount had been two thousand dollars. At the time Nickerson had given him the money, he had understood there were no strings attached to it, but he was going to call for an investigation. If it should appear that Nickerson was in any way interested in this zoning matter, it was all news to Crosset, and, as a matter of principle, Crosset intended to vote against any change in the zoning ordinance so that there could be no question of any money being paid to him in connexion with any pending ordinance.

The newspaper account went on to state that Drude Nickerson, who had been named by Crosset as having made a campaign contribution in an amount of two thousand dollars, was the same Drude Nickerson who was a witness in the Endicott murder case and, because of developments in the murder case, was at the moment unavailable for questioning.

The Santa Ana papers carried the story about a big eastern manufacturer looking for a suitable location and stated that, while it was rumoured Citrus Grove had been tentatively chosen by the manufacturer, there were now indications that property adjacent to Santa Ana was being considered for this big industrial expansion.

Stella Karis called me on the phone. She was so mad she could hardly talk. "What in hell have you done to me?" she asked. "Why, you double-crossing rat! You——!"

"Pipe down," I said. "I told you that any information you gave me wasn't confidential."

"Those may have been your words, but the way you told me you . . . you———"

"Listen," I said. "Keep your shirt on! The last time I saw you they were trying to put the squeeze on you for ten grand in addition to the fifteen you've already paid. You haven't heard any more about that additional squeeze, have you?"

"No," she admitted.

"You won't," I told her. "Sit tight. Don't be a damn fool. Go to a bank. Turn your property over to the bank for management and start painting nudes."

I hung up.

Another call came through. The voice was suave, polished.

"Mr. Lam?"

"Right."

"I am Homer Garfield, President of the Citrus Grove Chamber of Commerce."

"How are you, Mr. Garfield?"

"Very well, thank you, Mr. Lam. I have read various statements in the public Press concerning a potential expansion of Citrus Grove. The authority for those statements seems to have come from you."

"That's right."

"May I ask if you have some actual information?"

"You may."

"Do you?"

"I do."

"Can you tell me what it is?"

"No."

"Why?"

"I can't give you any information that I haven't given to the Press." I said. "However, I can tell you this: your evening paper carries a statement from Bailey Crosset about a campaign contribution made to him by Drude Nickerson. Why not get in touch with Drude Nickerson and find out about that campaign contribution? Why not interrogate the other members of the Trustees and see if campaign contributions have been made to them?"

"Nickerson is unavailable."

"What the hell?" I said. "You're representing the Chamber of Commerce. Who's going to tell you that Drude Nickerson is unavailable? Are you going to sit back and let a plant with a twenty-million-dollar annual payroll go to Santa Ana because your city is so damn crooked a concern can't get a reasonable change in your zoning ordinance? Are you going to let a bunch of cheap politicians keep twenty million dollars out of the pockets of your merchants because they want a two-bit contribution to election expenses?"

63

He cleared his throat. "That is a point I want to discuss, Mr. Lam. I want to find out more about that."

"Then you're calling the wrong person," I said. "Your district attorney holds an elective office. Your sheriff holds an elective office. Who the hell is going to make Drude Nickerson unavailable to you in a matter of this sort? You sit around there and twist your fingers and Santa Ana will wind up with the plant."

Again he cleared his throat. "May I ask where you got that twenty-million-dollar payroll figure, Mr. Lam?"

"Out of my head," I told him and hung up.

I went out and went to work chasing down the secretary Karl Carver Endicott had fired, the one who had gone to Mrs. Endicott with the story about John Ansel being sent out on a suicide expedition.

She wasn't hard to find.

Her name was Helen Manning. She wasn't bad looking, a blonde with blue eyes, a little heavy in the seat, but she certainly could play tunes on a typewriter.

She was working in an office where her employer didn't want her to talk on the job and she didn't want to talk on the job.

We wound up making a dinner date.

I went back to the office and checked in.

"There's a telegram," Elsie Brand told me.

It was from Barney Quinn. It said simply: "Good. Keep it up."

A reporter for the *Citrus Grove Clarion* called up. He wanted an interview.

"I can't talk about the murder case," I said. "You'll have to get in touch with Mr. Quinn and——"

His voice showed nerve strain. "To hell with the murder case," he said. "What about this factory?"

"Have you," I asked, "talked with the president of your Chamber of Commerce about that factory?"

"Have *I* talked with *him*!" the voice said. "*He's* talked with *us*!"

"Have you interviewed Drude Nickerson?" I asked.

"Now listen," he said, "what's all this about Drude Nickerson?"

"I simply asked if you'd interviewed him."

"No," he said shortly.

"I would suggest that you do so."

"Now look," he said, "something's happening. Another member of the Trustees has stated that *he* received a two-thousand-dollar contribution from Nickerson for campaign expenses. He insists that there was nothing that could possibly be a tie-in with any zoning ordinance. He says that he's going to investigate the facts in the case, and, if the money was in any way connected with any attempt to get him to vote for a change in the zoning ordinance, he's going to be against it."

"A fine bunch of Trustees you have!" I said.

"Is that sarcasm?"

"Is that sarcasm!" I said. "What are you talking about? The men have accepted campaign contributions. They state that if those contributions were connected in any way with pending ordinances they're going to vote against the ordinances."

"Now wait a minute," the reporter said. "Do you think that's fair?"

"What's fair?"

"For them to vote against an ordinance that way if the change in the ordinance might bring an influx of prosperity to this community?"

I said, "That's putting the matter on a dollars-and-cents basis. These Trustees have put it on a basis of personal integrity. I'm surprised that you'd even consider any financial argument in connexion with a decision involving the personal integrity of any member of your city council. I have no further comment to make."

I hung up.

I waited ten minutes and called Homer Garfield, President of the Citrus Grove Chamber of Commerce.

"I understand another councilman has admitted a two-thousand-dollar campaign contribution from Nickerson," I said.

His voice was cautious now. "Yes," he said, "that is true."

"Have you interviewed Nickerson?"

"As I have said earlier, Nickerson is not available."

"Are you," I asked, "going to let them continue to get away with that? Why should *he* make campaign contributions?"

He said drily, "Contributions of two thousands dollars are rather large for the office of city councilman."

"That's true," I said. "You might also ask Nickerson what other campaign contributions have been made. It would be interesting to know if the four thousand dollars represent the *only* campaign contribution he's made."

"May I ask what is your interest in the matter, Mr. Lam?"

"An interest in pure góvernment," I said. "An interest in upholding the ideals of our country. An interest in seeing that the merchants in your community don't look on you as a weak sister who lets Nickerson hide behind the district attorney's skirts simply because he's a witness in a murder case."

"The district attorney tells me that you are vitally interested in that murder case."

"He's telling you the truth."

"That you would like to see Nickerson discredited."

"I'd like to find out the facts," I said.

"He says that he refuses to permit his office to be jockeyed into the position of pulling chestnuts out of the fire for you."

"That means that you can't interview Nickerson?"

"He says it does."

"And that the grand jury won't be able to interview him?"

"I haven't questioned him about that."

"May I ask what your occupation is, Mr. Garfield?"

"I run a hardware store here."

"Any property in Santa Ana?"

"No."

"No vacant lots?"

"Well, I . . . I have some income-producing property in Santa Ana."

"I see," I said.

"Just what do you mean by that?"

"I was just asking. You're in quite a spot. I wouldn't want your job. If Citrus Grove gets the plant you don't get any credit. If Santa Ana gets it, everyone says you sold out. It's a tough spot to be in."

He ducked that question. "The only automobile company that has any reason to make such a move denies that it is interested in any such developments."

I said, "Remember the British officials who denied unequivocally that Britain was going off the gold standard?"

He thought that over.

I said, "If no company is planning to put in a big plant of that nature, how does it happen that at least two, and probably all of your Trustees got two thousand dollars payable towards their campaign expenses?"

"That," he blurted, "is the point that worries me."

"It should," I told him. "Let me ask you something else. Would any questions you might ask Nickerson about these campaign contributions have any effect whatever on his testimony in that Endicott murder case?"

"I don't see any reason why it should."

"Neither do I," I told him. "So why should the D.A. keep him out of circulation? I'll have to hang up now, Mr. Garfield. I have a dinner date. Good-bye."

CHAPTER THIRTEEN

HELEN MANNING had dolled herself up for the occasion. She had taste in selecting her garments. She'd been to the beauty parlour, and she had that indefinable something which enables some women to wear clothes so they look like Parisian gowns.

We had a couple of cocktails. She went through the motions of counting calories when it came to ordering dinner, but she surrendered easily to the waiter, the menu and my suggestions. She had a lobster cocktail, avocado-and-grapefruit salad, cream of tomato soup, filet mignon, a baked potato and mince pie à la mode.

We went to her apartment, and she brought out a bottle of crème de menthe. She turned the lights down because her eyes hurt after a long day in the office.

She crossed her knees. She had good legs. In the subdued light of the apartment she looked about twenty-two, and she had class.

When I'd seen her by daylight banging away at the type-writer, in the office where she was working, she looked thirty-five and tired.

"What is it you want to know?" she asked.

I said, "You worked for Karl Carver Endicott?"

"Yes."

"In what capacity?"

"As a confidential secretary."

"How was he to work for?"

"Splendid!"

"A gentleman?"

"Wonderful!"

"Anything personal?"

"Certainly not," she said acidly. "The relationship was on a business basis. If he hadn't been enough of a gentleman to have kept it on that basis, I was enough of a lady to have insisted upon it."

"You learned a good deal about his affairs?"

"Yes."

"How about his honesty?"

"He was absolutely, scrupulously honest. It was a very fine position."

"Why did you quit?"

"For personal reasons."

"What were they?"

"I resigned."

"Why?"

"The atmosphere of the office had changed in a way."

"In what way?"

"It's difficult to describe. I didn't care for some of the other girls in the office. I could get a job anywhere. I didn't have to put up with an environment I didn't like. I quit the job."

"Any hard feelings?"

"Certainly not. Mr. Endicott gave me a very fine letter of recommendation. I can show that to you if you wish."

"I'd like to see it."

She went to the bedroom and came out after a while with a letter on the stationery of the Endicott Enterprises. It was a swell letter. It recommended Helen Manning as a competent secretary who had been with him for years. She was leaving voluntarily and he regretted losing her.

"Now then," I said, folding the letter, "shortly afterwards you went to talk with Mrs. Endicott, didn't you?"

"*I* did?" she exclaimed incredulously.

"You."

"Certainly *not!*" she said. "I had seen Mrs. Endicott in the office once or twice. I knew who she was, and of course I exchanged the time of day with her, but that's all."

"You didn't talk with her at all after you had quit your position?"

"I may have said good morning if I saw her in the street, but I don't even remember that."

"You didn't give her a ring on the telephone and ask her to tell you where you could meet her because you had something to tell her?"

"Certainly not."

"That's fine," I said. "Would you mind giving me an affidavit to that effect?"

"Why should I?"

"So I can report the true facts to my employers and spike a rumour that is going around."

"But I see no reason for making any such statement."

"It's true, isn't it?"

"Of course it's true. I wouldn't lie."

"Then you can make an affidavit."

She was silent for several seconds. Then she asked abruptly, "How did you know about this?"

"About what?"

"About my going to Mrs. Endicott."

"Don't be silly," I said. "You didn't go to her. You're going to give me an affidavit to that effect."

"All right," she said savagely. "I went to her! I told her things I thought she should know."

"What was the trouble with Karl Endicott?" I asked.

"Everything," she said. "After all I'd done for him! I gave

him the best years of my life. I was loyal. I was absolutely devoted to him. I put up with things that ... I closed my eyes to things ... I wouldn't permit the slightest thought of his chicanery even to enter my mind. And then he got this little hussy in. It wouldn't have been so bad if she could have done the work. She couldn't even type. She didn't know straight up. She was just a little strumpet who was twisting him around her finger, and——"

"And you made a scene?" I asked.

"I did *not* make a scene," she said. "I simply told him that if he wanted to keep a mistress, he should keep her in an apartment and not jeopardize the business by trying to keep her in the office. I also told him that if I was going to be the chief secretary I wanted it understood that *I* was the chief secretary, that I didn't want some little tart who had a face and a figure and no brains telling *me* what to do."

"So he fired you?"

She began to cry.

"He fired you?" I asked.

"He fired me, goddam him!" she said between sobs.

"That's better," I told her. "You went to Mrs. Endicott. What did you tell her?"

"I told her what had happened. Karl Endicott sent John Ansel and another man into the Amazon jungles. He knew that it was legalized murder. He wanted to get rid of both of them."

"When did you know this?"

"I knew it when I talked with Mrs. Endicott."

"How long before?"

"Not very long before."

"Why not?"

"Because ... because I wouldn't let myself even question his motives."

"How did he know what they were going to encounter in the Amazon?"

"Some other people had been up in that same territory. That had been a *bona fide* expedition. The people had been killed. Endicott knew they had been killed."

"How?"

"It was an expedition by another oil company and Endicott got the information on that."

"How?"

"By correspondence."

"Where's the correspondence?"

"In his files, I guess."

"You didn't take it out when you left?"

"No, I wish I had."

"You have no photostats?"

"No."

"No way of proving what you know?"

"Only that I saw the letters. I typed some of his letters of inquiry."

"Did Endicott make any settlement when you left? Any sort of property adjustment?"

"Why should he?"

"Did he?"

"No."

"You're dependent on your salary?"

"I'm a working girl."

I sized her up. Six years ago she had been quite a dish. She was still a good-looking babe. Then she had been twenty-nine. Now she was thirty-five. She could type like nobody's business.

I said, "It would be unfortunate if some of this came out."

"In what way?"

I said, "Employers don't like secretaries who become temperamental and go to wives with stories of the husband's business."

She thought that over.

I looked at my watch.

"Gosh, Helen," I said, "I've got to rush on. I'm working on this Endicott case, and I've got a million and one things to do. It was perfectly swell of you to give me an evening of your time."

"Thank you for a wonderful dinner, Donald," she said.

She came to the door with me. I kissed her good night but it wasn't much of a kiss. She was preoccupied with her thoughts, and she was worried to beat hell.

CHAPTER FOURTEEN

MAYOR TABER was a man in his middle fifties with heavy jowls, thick lips, cold grey eyes, and a habit of talking in rapid spurts making his words sound like bursts of machine-gun fire.

Cooper Hale was short, fat and quiet. He looked me over, then turned his eyes away, then looked me over, then turned his eyes away.

Bertha performed the introductions, and both men shook hands. Taber did the talking.

"Very unfortunate publicity, very unfortunate indeed! It seems to have emanated from this office. Now I don't know what your sources of information are, Lam, and I don't give a damn. All I can say is that it has been insinuated the city government of Citrus Grove has been asleep at the switch, and we've let some stupid zoning ordinance stand in the way of development."

He stopped for a moment, took a deep breath, went on rattling out the words. "I don't like it. That's not the way to fight. If you have any legitimate grievance against the city, come down to Citrus Grove and tell us about it. I don't know what you're trying to do. I do know you're mixed in this Endicott murder case, and while I'm not prepared to make any direct accusations in public—as yet—I can't get it out of my mind that there must be a tie-in."

"Meaning the information I had is false?" I asked.

"Of course it's false."

"What about Crosset's campaign fund?" I asked.

"Well now *there* is a matter which is rather unfortunate. I'm very friendly with Crosset, and I respect and admire the man enormously. He's a man of upright integrity. He has such rigid principles, such high standards of honour that anything that would cast the faintest smirch on his character would be magnified in his mind. I'm terribly sorry it happened."

"So is Crosset," I said.

"He's entitled to accept campaign contributions provided he acts in good faith."

"That's right."

"Well, then why bring the matter up?"

"He resigned, didn't he?"

"He resigned."

"Why?"

"Because, as I have explained to you, his standards of honour are so high that he would lean over backwards."

"What about the others?"

"What others?"

"The others who had two thousand dollars donated to their campaign funds."

"Do you *know* that any of the others did?"

"I understand one of the others stated a similar contribution had been made."

"Well, what's wrong with that?"

"Nothing."

"Then why bring it up?"

"I didn't."

"You asked the question."

"I was trying to familiarize myself with the situation."

Hale shifted his position, raised his eyes to look at me. "After all," he said, "*you* may not be in an invulnerable position yourself, Lam."

"In what way?"

"Many ways."

"Name them."

"I don't have to."

"Name one."

"I'm simply making a statement."

"All right. You've made it. Now back it up."

"We didn't come here to fight," Taber said.

"What did you come here for?"

"We'd like to have the co-operation of your firm."

"In what way?"

"You have been talking with the Press."

"Any objection?"

"We feel some of the statements that have been made to the Press are irresponsible."

"Would you like to see Santa Ana get a big factory away from Citrus Grove?"

"Certainly not. And, for your information, there's no likelihood anything of that sort can happen."

"Want to bet?"

"I am not a betting man. I am, however, a businessman."

"You're a politician?"

"I have been in politics."

"And you expect to be in politics?"

"Possibly."

I said, "This company wants to come to Citrus Grove. It has its location picked out. It wants a reasonable amount of co-operation from the city government. Now of course I don't know anything about what the newspapers are going to say. I do know that one of the reporters has an idea."

"What?"

"The idea that some person with powerful political connexions who owns land in Citrus Grove wants to change the location of this factory and is stalling around over a zoning ordinance change hoping he can learn the identity of the manufacturer and steal the deal."

"That's absolutely ridiculous! That's absurd! That's utterly false!" Hale said.

"I was merely commenting about an idea one of the reporters has," I told him.

"If you can tell me which one, I'll punch his nose."

"Why?" I asked.

"Because there's nothing to it."

"Then *why* should *you* punch his nose? What's it to *you*?"

Hale said nothing.

Taber said, "What Mr. Hale means is that a publication of that sort of a story, accompanied by a lot of innuendoes, might reflect upon him personally."

"You mean *he* has property in Citrus Grove?"

"I have always been a strong believer in the future of Citrus Grove," Hale said unctuously. "I have made money by a series of fortunate real estate investments, which have backed my faith in the growth of the community. I have made considerable personal sacrifices to help this community."

"That's the spirit!" I said.

"It is indeed," Taber agreed.

"All right," Bertha said, "this crap isn't getting us anywhere. What do you want?"

"Mr. Nickerson is a witness in the Endicott murder case," Taber said.

I said nothing.

"So is Mr. Hale," Taber went on.

"Well?" I asked.

"And *you* are interested in the Endicott murder case," Taber said.

"We're working on it," I told him.

"Ansel doesn't stand a chance! Not a single chance in the world! The case against him is dead open-and-shut."

"Doubtless the district attorney thinks it is," I said. "Mr. Quinn, who is the attorney for the defence, has other ideas."

"It is a case where the citizens of the community feel greatly incensed," Taber said. "That community spirit will manifest itself throughout the trial. In fact, some of the jurors will undoubtedly be from the vicinity of Citrus Grove. The district attorney will demand the death penalty and I don't think there is the slightest chance but what Ansel will be sent to the gas chamber."

I said nothing.

"Now," Taber went on, "we are prepared to co-operate. If, as I rather suspect, much of the motivation back of these rumours which have been appearing in the Press is due to a desire to distract attention from the Endicott case and involve certain witnesses, it *might* be that you are resorting to the wrong tactics. You *might* make more actual progress by trying to co-operate instead of trying to tear down."

"In what way?"

"The district attorney is not an unreasonable man. As it happens he is a friend of mine. I feel certain that he would be amenable to reason."

"In what way?"

"I feel quite certain that if Ansel should plead guilty the district attorney would take into consideration the fact that a great deal of expense had been saved the county and no attempt would be made to try to get the judge to impose the death penalty. In fact, it *might* well be that the district attorney himself would ask for a life sentence. I am not in a position to state. I don't represent the district attorney. I am only exploring the situation."

"I see."

"It *might* even be that Ansel could plead guilty to second-degree murder or manslaughter."

I said, "I don't think Mr. Quinn would be interested in such a deal. It is Mr. Quinn's opinion that John Ansel is absolutely innocent."

"That's a completely cockeyed assumption. It disregards the cold, hard, evidentiary facts."

"I'm not as yet too familiar with the facts," I said. "We're working on the case."

"Well, when you get familiar with the facts," Taber said, getting to his feet, "you can get in touch with me. You can always find me in my office at Citrus Grove. And I may state that I'm always glad to do anything which will advance the economic interests of my fair city."

"Then you'd better get busy with that zoning ordinance," I said.

"What do you mean?"

"If five members of the Trustees got two thousand dollars apiece from Drude Nickerson," I said, "it's rather remarkable that someone would be that interested.

"Now," I went on, "*I* have a *personal* theory. My theory is that members of the Trustees each received two thousand dollars as a contribution to their campaign fund, but they didn't receive it with the understanding that they were going to vote in *favour* of changing a zoning ordinance. I think they received the money with the understanding that Mr. Nickerson would be very, very happy to see the zoning ordinance remain unchanged so that the location of the new factory could be diverted to some property held by a friend of his.

74

"I can't give you all the names as yet, but I hope to have them by this time tomorrow."

"You're working on this?" Taber asked.

"Certainly I'm working on it."

"Professionally?"

I said, "I hope I'm not doing it amateurishly."

"You *could* get into trouble over this thing, you know."

"Sure, I could. So could a lot of other people. I wonder if Mr. Crosset reported the two thousand dollars that he received on his income tax."

"You don't have to report contributions made for campaign expenditures," Taber said.

I grinned at him.

"At least, I don't think you do," he amended.

I kept on grinning.

Hale said, "We've done everything we can do here, Charles. We've offered to co-operate. The district attorney is my friend. I'm willing to do what I can, but I want people to meet me halfway."

Taber nodded. "All right," he said, "we just dropped in for a visit to get acquainted. We thought you should appreciate our position."

"I'm damned certain you should appreciate ours," I told him.

"You'll hear from us again," he said, and both men walked out without shaking hands.

When the door had closed, Bertha's eyes were snapping cold light like the diamonds on her fingers.

"Donald," she said, "What the hell are you trying to do? You've insulted those men. You've virtually made accusations of double-dealing."

"Did it impress you that way?" I asked.

"It certainly did."

"Then in all likelihood it impressed them the same way."

"Do you have any idea what you're talking about in this case?"

"Sure I do. Nickerson got fifteen grand from a Stella Karis. She wanted some zoning ordinances changed because there was a factory that wanted to locate on some of her land.

"Nickerson found out about it. Hale knew about it. Hale had some land that he wanted to lease to the factory. He didn't want Stella Karis in the picture.

"So Hale decided to bribe the councilmen to sit tight and not change the zoning ordinance. However, Hale was constitutionally opposed to putting up any money, so he and Nickerson worked out a swell double cross by which they got Stella Karis to put up the money ostensibly for the purpose of influencing the council to *grant* the zoning ordinance, but Nickerson used that money as a bribe to get the city councilmen to *leave the zoning ordinance the way it was.*

"By the time the people of Citrus Grove get the idea that a big factory offering employment to thousands of men went elsewhere simply because some politician wanted to get in on the ground floor, it's going to make quite a little——"

Bertha interrupted to say, "I hope the hell you know what you're doing."

"So do I," I told her. "Public opinion is quite a thing when it gets aroused."

"Well, you're sure as hell arousing it. They say that people are gathered in little knots down in Citrus Grove, and aren't talking about anything else—just the murder and the automobile factory."

At three-thirty-five o'clock that afternoon the city council of Citrus Grove met in a special session and took steps to change the zoning ordinance so that the property belonging to Stella Karis was zoned for a manufacturing district.

With the passing of the ordinance, the *Citrus Grove Clarion* assured its readers that the industrial expansion for which the farsighted officials had been quietly campaigning during the last few weeks was assured.

Drude Nickerson remained "unavailable" for questioning.

Stella Karis telephoned twice while I was out. She left a message with Elsie Brand. Elsie Brand took it down in her shorthand book and relayed it to me when I came in. It was to the effect that Miss Karis had said she would like to see me, that she "simply couldn't express her gratitude in words".

I let it go at that.

CHAPTER FIFTEEN

A LARGE part of the detective work in a murder trial consists of getting the backgrounds of the trial jurors. As soon as the case was set for trial, Bertha and I went to work on the venire from which the twelve jurors who were to try the case would be selected.

Bertha worked on the older men and the older women. I worked on the younger ones.

It was of course unethical and would have been a contempt of court to have talked with these people about the case, to have shadowed them so that they knew they were being shadowed, or to have engaged in any other activities that might be deemed to influence them.

However, there was no law against chatting casually with some of their friends or digging into the records and finding out where they had acted as jurors before, what kind of cases they were, and how they had voted.

It was a long tedious job but in the end we had a pretty good collection of condensed biographies.

Barney Quinn took these biographies and broke them down into short summaries. Then he took the short summaries and broke them down into an elaborate code. A short, straight mark at the top of a square opposite a prospective juror's name meant he was honest and upright, but acceptable. If the mark leaned to the left, it meant he was so upright he'd lean over backwards. If the mark was down at the bottom of the square, it meant the man was obstinate, pigheaded, and bigoted. If the mark was horizontal, it meant he would lie down when the going got tough.

In between times I'd keep checking on the facts.

The day before the trial Stell Karis gave me a ring.

"You don't ever come to see me, Donald."

"I'm busy day and night."

"You have to eat."

"I don't eat. I gulp."

"I could watch you gulp. I have something to tell you."

"About what?"

"About the case you're working on."

"What about it?"

"Mr. Hale has been to see me."

"The deuce he has!"

"Uh-huh, several times."

"What does he want?"

She laughed seductively. "I'll tell you, but not over the 'phone."

"Honestly, Stella, I haven't the time right at the moment for——"

"This concerns a witness in the case."

"I'll see you."

"When?"

"How about tonight?"

"Dinner?"

"Make it after dinner," I said. "I have a dinner date. Is nine o'clock too late?"

"No, come on it. I'll be waiting."

I put in the day cleaning up the last of the jury list, getting things ready, and dropped in to see Stella about five minutes to nine.

As she opened the door and bent towards me, the neckline of her dress disclosed curves, and as she turned to lead the way into her apartment, a tantalizing bit of leg showed from a generous split in the tight-fitting skirt.

We had coffee. Then we had liqueurs. Then she said, "Donald, Mr. Hale wants to manage my properties."

"How nice!" I said.

"You told me I should have some bank——"

"Look here," I said, "are you so absolutely crazy that you would turn your properties over to anything Hale was managing?"

"He's organizing an investment company."

"How very, very nice—for Cooper Hale!"

She said, "He's very friendly. He hates you."

"I can bear up," I told her.

"He thinks that I hate you, too."

"He does?"

"Uh-huh. I told him that you never came to see me any more. He wanted to pump me about you."

"Go ahead."

"And he told me something that he said no one knew anything about."

"What?"

"A rancher by the name of Thomas Victor," she said. "You remember the night Endicott was murdered?"

"Uh-huh."

"You know Mrs. Endicott was supposed to have been at a gasoline station just at nine o'clock and the fatal shot was fired at exactly nine o'clock. Well, Thomas Victor was at that gasoline station at seven minutes to nine that night trying to get some gasoline and the station was already closed. He thinks the man who was running the station either closed up early or else his watch was fast."

"Or else Victor's watch was slow," I said.

"Victor says it wasn't. I thought I'd let you know, Donald."

"Thanks."

"Is it important?" she asked.

"That," I said, "is probably not as important as the fact that Hale saw fit to tell you about it."

"Why?"

"That," I said, "is something I don't know. Anyhow I'll check. How's the factory deal coming along?"

"Oh, they've signed the lease, and—— You know something, Donald? You were right. It wasn't a novelty company at all. When it came right down to brass tacks, it turned out to be a big roller-bearing company that makes a line of roller bearings in the East. It wanted this as a plant to take care of their western business."

"Uh-huh."

"Aren't you thrilled?"

"Are you?"

"I'm making a lot of money out of it."

"Do you like making money?"

"Frankly, Donald, I don't. I would like to go back to drawing and painting. I suppose I'm only a second-rate artist, but it's creative. It's my life!

"I like the people I meet who are in that field. I can talk with them about light, perspective—things like that—and they not only know what I mean but we're talking about something worthwhile.

"Nowadays it seems to be all a question of leases and securities and net returns and all of that kind of stuff.

"Donald, would *you* manage an investment company for me?"

"No."

"Why?"

"Because I'd be working for you."

"Is there anything wrong with that?"

"Yes. It would be like running around on a leash. To hell with that stuff. I'm doing all right the way I am."

"I was afraid you'd say that." She thought for a while.

"Cooper Hale doesn't feel that way," she said at length.

"*He* wouldn't!"

"Do you think if he should organize an investment company that I should let him manage my securities? He guarantees me a very nice income."

I said, "My only advice to you is to put your securities in the trust department of a reputable bank. Let them manage things for you so that you get a low but safe yield. Get rid of all your real estate holdings and everything that requires personal management. Put the money into a portfolio of blue ribbon securities. Then start painting. Go to Europe and study art over there if you want to. Try to do something really worth while."

"Yes, I suppose so," she said.

"Been married?" I asked her.

"Yes. I told you that that first night I met you in Reno."

"What happened to the marriage?" I asked.

She followed the design on the davenport with the tip of her forefinger. "It broke up. I'm a divorcee."

"Why didn't it work?"

"I don't like to be owned. I think that people who have a truly creative temperament chafe at the idea of ... of being possessed.

"I think that's the reason actors and actresses can stand matrimony for only so long at a stretch. People talk about the immorality of Hollywood and it really isn't immorality, Donald. It's just something bigger than you are. It doesn't keep you from falling in love, but after the love part gets to a point where you try to conform to conventional standards and you feel someone owns you, you start fighting, not against the person, but against the idea of being possessed."

"Want to get married again?" I asked.

"Is this a proposal?" she asked me.

"No, it's a question."

"Not particularly. I think there *are* some people I could ... well, sometimes I have symptoms of falling in love."

I said, "You're a great mark for a fortune hunter right now. How much property do you have?"

"That's none of your damn business."

"Keep it that way."

"What way?"

"It's none of anyone's business how much you have. If you want my advice, put your property in securities, go back to New York and live on two hundred dollars a month. Make up your mind that, no matter what happens, you won't spend more than two hundred dollars a month for anything."

"Do you know I've been thinking of doing that very thing."

"Think of it some more," I told her. "And now I'm on my way. I'm busy."

"I don't see anything of you any more," she pouted.

"I don't see anything of myself," I told her, "except for the few brief minutes I'm looking at my face in the mirror when I'm shaving in the morning."

"After this case is over, will I see you some, Donald?"

"I don't know."

She laughed and said, "You're worse than I am. *You* don't want to be possessed. *You* don't want anyone to have any strings on you."

"You may be right," I told her, "but right now I'm going to have to hit the hay because I have a hard day ahead of me."

I yawned a couple of times, kissed her good night, got the hell out of there and called Barney Quinn on the phone.

Quinn's voice was tense and urgent. I started to tell him that I'd picked up a live lead, but I never had the chance. "Look, Donald," he said, "I've been trying to locate you all afternoon. How soon can you get down here?"

"Right away. Bertha and I have been out all day checking jurors."

"Okay," he said. "I couldn't reach either of you. Bring Bertha."

"That bad?" I asked.

"Worse," he said.

I said, "I can tell you a little something about the other side of the case. They're checking on the time element of that gas station."

"What gas station? Oh, I get it. Well, that's a minor matter now. Come on down."

"It may take a little while to round up Bertha," I said.

"Then come on down, and let Bertha come later. This is important. All hell's loose."

CHAPTER SIXTEEN

BERTHA heaved, grunted, groaned and cussed when she got my call, but she was ready by the time I drove by and we made time to Santa Ana.

Quinn was locked in his office. There were circles under his eyes. The place was filled with cigarette smoke, the ash trays were cluttered up with half-smoked cigarettes. He was jittery.

Bertha strode across the office, heaved herself into a chair, said, "Young man, you're making a goddam wreck out of yourself."

"It's the case that's making a wreck out of me," he said. "I've sent for Elizabeth Endicott. She should be here any moment. If it's okay by you, I'll wait and tell you the sad news after she gets here, then I won't have to tell it twice."

"Is it sad?" I asked.

"It's sad," he said, and crushed a half-smoked cigarette in the ash tray.

"I can add to it," I told him.

"All right. Go ahead. We may as well catch it all at once. We——"

Knuckles sounded on the door.

Quinn strode across the office, opened the door, and Mrs. Endicott said, "Good evening, Barney."

"Come on in, Betty," he told her. "I'm sorry I had to call a night conference, but the fat's in the fire."

"What fat?" she asked. "And what fire?"

"Sit down," Quinn said.

She dropped into a chair.

Quinn faced her. "You told me a great story," he said, "about John Ansel being psychic, about knowing when he got in the house that you weren't there, about having an idea that Karl Endicott was going to murder him. You said that when Karl stepped in the other room, John Ansel had a sudden feeling that Karl was getting ready to kill him and then plant a gun on him."

"That's the truth," she said.

"Is that the truth?" he asked, "or is that the story that you thought should be told, and you've been drilling it into John Ansel so that he would tell it that way?"

Her face was without expression, "It's the truth."

"No, it isn't the truth," Quinn said. "It's the story John told me the first couple of times, but we're getting down to brass tacks now. He's going to go on the witness stand, and when he goes on the witness stand he's going to be cross-examined by a mighty smart district attorney."

Elizabeth Endicott said, "John Ansel is truthful. His story is founded on fact."

"Founded on fact, my eye!" Quinn blazed. "John went down to Citrus Grove intending to face Karl Endicott with the facts. He intended to kill Karl. He had a gun with him. Karl was the one who was psychic. Karl took one look at John and manœuvred him into the upstairs den, and then excused himself for a moment and went into the other room. It was a bedroom. You were in there."

"*I* was?" she asked.

Quinn nodded. "You said one thing that was true in the story you told. John had been down in the jungle. He'd been living away from civilisation. He'd been fighting a battle with life and death where his senses had to be alert.

"You were in that room. When Karl opened the door, the perfume that you use came to John's nostrils. Then Karl closed the door. When he did that, he said something to you in a low voice.

"Suddenly John realized that you were Karl Endicott's wife, that you'd been living with him as his wife. A feeling of revulsion possessed him. He started to become nauseated. The gun that he was holding in his hand he pitched out of the window. It fell in the thick hedge. He felt he was going to be ill. He dashed out of the door and ran down the stairs, and out into the night air."

Quinn quit talking, stood with his feet apart facing her, the accusation in his manner hitting her with almost a physical impact.

She didn't cry. She wilted. She looked at him steadily but she seemed to keep getting smaller.

Finally she said, "I told him he must never, never tell that story."

Quinn said, "Ansel is a poor liar, when you start ripping into him. He doesn't like conflict. I'd always accepted his story at face value, but we're going to trial tomorrow, and he's going to have to get on the stand. They're going to rip him to pieces with cross-examination. So this morning I decided to cross-examine him myself just to see how he'd stand up."

There was a moment of tense, dramatic silence.

"I found out," Quinn said bitterly and turned away.

"I'm sorry," Elizabeth Endicott said, dry-eyed and steady-voiced.

"You should be," Quinn snapped at her.

"*Were* you in the room?" I asked Elizabeth Endicott.

"No," she said quickly but without emphasis.

"That's a hell of a denial," Quinn said. "You're going to be on the stand. Put some feeling into it."

"*No!*" she said.

"That's better," Quinn said.

I said, "Your alibi depends on a man by the name of Walden who was closing his service station at nine o'clock."

She said, "It's a good alibi."

I said, "The district attorney has a rancher by the name of Thomas Victor who drove past that service station at seven minutes to nine. He wanted to get gasoline. The station was closed."

She moistened her lips with the tip of her tongue. "Victor's watch was wrong."

Barney said, "Good Lord, Lam! There can't be anything wrong with *that* alibi. Walden testified at the inquest, and they really poured it to him. Victor is the one who's making the mistake."

I kept looking at Elizabeth Endicott. "She's playing poker with us," I said to Quinn.

Quinn whirled back to face her. "Betty, we're going to trial tomorrow. You can't afford to lie to us. We're your friends. We're the ones who are faced with the responsibility of saving everything you want in life. If you lie to us, you are cutting your own throat. Tell us the truth."

"I've told it to you," she said.

Quinn turned to me. "What do you think, Donald?"

"I think she's lying."

Bertha Cool said, "Donald, you can't——"

"The hell I can't," I interrupted. "Look up Section 258 of the Probate Code, Barney. Read it to her."

"What section is that?" Bertha asked.

"Section 258," I said.

Elizabeth Endicott looked at me. "Are you a lawyer?" she asked.

"He used to be," Bertha Cool said. "He's had a legal education. He's one smart little bastard. If you're lying, dearie, you'd better get it off your chest."

Quinn turned the pages of the Probate Code.

"Got it?" I asked.

"Yes," he said.

"Read it to her," I said.

Quinn read the section. " '*No person convicted of the murder or voluntary manslaughter of the decedent shall be entitled to succeed to any portion of the estate; but the portion thereof to which he would otherwise be entitled to succeed goes to the other persons entitled thereto under the provisions of this chapter.*' "

Quinn looked at Mrs. Endicott, then he looked at me. His face was pasty. "My God!" he said.

"Go ahead," I told Elizabeth Endicott, "let's have the truth."

Her eyes met mine. "You're working for me," she said. "You have no right to say I'm lying."

"The hell I haven't! I'm working *for* you. I'd like to salvage something before it's too late."

"I wasn't in the house when the shot was fired," she said.

"Where were you?"

"On the road to San Diego."

"Let's try it again," I told her.

"All right," she said. "I'll tell you this. I *was* on the road to San Diego but I can't prove it. Walden, who ran the service station, *was* mistaken. He thought he closed up at nine o'clock. He hadn't wound his watch that day. It stopped about seven o'clock. He tuned in his radio in order to get the time. The programme was over at seven-fifteen. *He* thought it was over at seven-thirty. He set his watch fifteen minutes fast. He didn't realize it until after he had testified at the inquest. He was absolutely positive his watch was right. He said at the inquest that he had set his watch by the radio less than two hours before he closed. Everyone took it for granted that he had set his watch with a time signal. He hadn't. He'd set it with a programme. He'd made a mistake of fifteen minutes on the programme."

"He found this out?" I asked.

"Yes. He found it out after the inquest. But Bruce Walden has confidence in me. I told him that it wouldn't make any difference, that I actually *was* on my way to San Diego and he believed me. So he has never said anything."

"Where's Bruce Walden now?" I asked.

"He was running a service station then. Now he's a gasoline distributor for the entire county."

Quinn looked at me.

I said, "They have this man Victor. Victor's positive the station was closed at seven minutes to nine when he drove by."

Elizabeth Endicott said, "If they should start digging, Mrs. Walden would also testify that her husband was mistaken. He got home at five minutes past nine. He couldn't have done that if he actually closed the station at nine. She took it for granted he'd closed up early. Nothing was said. It wasn't until after the inquest that she began to put two and two together. She asked him about setting his watch. He told her how it had happened. She's the one who pointed out to him that he was fifteen minutes off on the time."

Quinn looked at me and threw up his hands.

Bertha Cool said, "Fry me for an oyster!"

"All right," I told Quinn. "We'll start from here. One of the first things to do is to find that gun before the D.A. finds it. Remember this: the D.A.'s in a spot. He's prosecuting John Ansel for first-degree murder. He doesn't want to back up and dismiss. Even if he could *prove* Walden closed that station fifteen minutes early he *still* hasn't proven Elizabeth Endicott guilty of killing her husband. That's bothering him right now. That's raising hell with his thinking.

"We're going out and find that gun if it's still there."

"But don't you see," Barney Quinn said, "when Ansel gets on the stand he's going to have to tell the truth. He can't lie successfully, and now that I know his story, I can't put him on and let him tell a lie. He has to tell about that gun."

I said, "He doesn't have to get on the stand."

"If we don't put him on the stand, we're licked," Barney said.

"No," I told him. "We'll let the district attorney play into our hands."

"How?"

"We'll give him a witness."

"Who?"

"Helen Manning."

"Who's she?"

"She's a discharged secretary who came to Elizabeth Endicott and told her what a heel her husband was. The woman who made Elizabeth Endicott think about that Karl had deliberately sent John to his death. She's the woman who made Elizabeth Endicott think about killing her husband. She's the woman who first put the idea into Elizabeth's head."

Elizabeth Endicott sat perfectly still, her face an absolute mask. "What are you trying to do?" she asked. "Send *me* to the gas chamber?"

"We're trying to get the district attorney straddling a barbed-wire fence," I said, "one foot on one side, one foot on the other."

"You can't do it with that guy. He's smart," Quinn warned.

"All right," I said, "what are *you* going to do with him?"

Quinn didn't have the answer to that one.

I turned to Elizabeth Endicott. "There's only one thing for us to do. We don't dare use flashlights. We can't make the search by daylight or someone would tip the police off. Cooper Hale owns the property next to your estate so we'll have to wait until well after midnight. We'll go out to your house. We'll ease out of the side door. Then we've got to get down on our hands and knees and search every inch of that hedge by feeling."

"But what will we do if we find it?" Barney Quinn asked.

"*We'll* keep it," I said.

"It will be evidence," Quinn pointed out. "It's a crime to conceal evidence. It's unprofessional conduct. They could disbar me for that."

I grinned at him. "You won't be there, Barney. Tomorrow be sure to ask me if we found a gun in the hedge. Come on, Bertha, let's go. We'll see you at your place in a couple of hours, Mrs. Endicott. Leave the back door open for us. You can fortify us with coffee and assure us the coast is clear."

CHAPTER SEVENTEEN

IT was a dark night. High fog was drifting in from the ocean and there was a lot of humidity in the air.

Bertha Cool and I were down on our hands and knees on the damp grass, crawling along the hedge, our fingers digging through every inch of the soil.

"Why did you tell Betty Endicott to stay inside?" she asked.

"For one reason, we can't trust her," I said. "For another reason, in case anybody comes she can give us a signal."

"I've ruined a dress, a pair of nylons and broken two finger-nails," Bertha Cool said.

"That's nothing," I said. "You may be ruining your professional career."

"Why the hell do we do this?"

"It's a service we give our clients."

"I never did anything like this before you came along," Bertha said. "It wasn't until you teamed up with me that we started getting into all these damn scrapes."

"You never made money before," I told her. "Shut up and get busy. Don't just skim along the surface. Work your fingers down deep into the soil. The thing has been out here for years, and it'll be pretty well covered."

"How come no one's found it?" she asked.

"No one's looked. The gardener puts water on the hedge. He trims it once in a while. The hedge is so thick it keeps weeds from growing underneath and he's never spaded it up to do a decent job of it. He's cut sod around the edges and thrown dirt into the centre. He's probably covered the thing up years ago."

Bertha ripped out a string of cuss words.

"What's the matter?"

"I've torn my dress and scratched my face. Donald, why the hell can't we have a flashlight on this job?"

"We can't let anyone know what's going on. The police may be keeping the place under surveillance. Hale lives next door."

Bertha grunted, groaned, heaved around on her hands and knees. She cussed me up one side and down the other, and then my fingers struck something.

"Wait a minute, Bertha!" I said. "I think ... it's either a stone or ... okay, this is it. It's the gun!"

"Well, thank God," Bertha said. "It's about time!" She heaved herself to her feet. "I don't know how the hell I'm going to get into my apartment house. If the doorman gets a look at me, he'll think I've been stealing chickens."

"Tell him he's underestimating you," I told her. "Tell him

you've been compounding a felony. Stealing chickens is a misdemeanour."

"Well," Bertha said, "let's go tell Elizabeth Endicott, and I suppose we should telephone Barney Quinn."

"No," I said.

"No what?"

"We'll tell Elizabeth Endicott we searched the whole damn hedge and couldn't find anything," I told her. "We tell Barney Quinn the same thing."

"Sometimes," Bertha said with feeling, "I wish to hell I'd never seen you."

88

CHAPTER EIGHTEEN

THERE was one thing wrong with the story John Dittmar Ansel had told Barney Quinn.

The gun was pretty badly rusted. I couldn't even break the cylinder open without subjecting the gun to a lot of treatment designed to remove rust. But by using my flashlight after I'd cleaned out some of the dirt from the barrel, I could see, despite the rust, that the shell in line with the barrel had been fired. The beam of the flashlight very plainly showed the empty cartridge case. The other five cartridges had bullets in them.

It was one hell of a mess.

The case started on schedule. We droned through getting the jury empanelled.

Barney Quinn had our notes. He had us sitting in court where we could be consulted, but the guy had lost heart. He was like a man being dragged into the execution chamber. He carefully refrained from asking us anything about the gun.

During the noon recess, I took him off to one side where there were no reporters around and handed it to him straight from the shoulder.

"This is the kind of stuff that separates the men from the boys," I told him. "You're in this case as an attorney representing a defendant who is charged with murder. The punishment for murder is death. The jurors are watching the district attorney and the jurors are watching you. You look like a man who's defending a guilty client. That's not fair to you and it's not fair to your client. Get the hell in there and fight. Don't fight as though you had your back to the wall, but fight with the smiling confidence of a man who is representing an innocent defendant."

"I'm not that good an actor," Quinn said.

"You'd better start learning then," I told him.

He did a little better in the afternoon.

Using the information we had dug up for him, Quinn knew everything there was to know about the jurors. The danger, of course, lay in the fact that the panel would be exhausted. Then the judge would have to order a special venire, and Quinn would have a list of names about which he knew nothing.

Mortimer Irvine, the district attorney, was a tall, good-looking, dignified man with wavy dark hair, broad shoulders, slim waist and an air of distinction.

Irvine was unmarried, considered one of the most eligible bachelors in the country, and he loved to get impressionable young women on a jury. He'd also go for the older, white-haired, matronly type. He didn't like the horny-handed ranchers.

The impressionable young women looked on him as they'd look on a matinee idol. They'd listen to his arguments and bring in a verdict of conviction, walk out of a court-room and say to each other, "Wasn't he just wonderful!"

The older women said Irvine reminded them of what "Jimmy" would have been like if "Jimmy" had only lived. "Jimmy" had always wanted to be a lawyer.

Some of the horny-handed old ranchers would look at Irvine's carefully combed hair, gaze into his soulful eyes, and return a verdict for the defendant.

Barney Quinn had made up his jury list with the idea of keeping as many of the young women as possible off the jury. Irvine had made up his jury list with the idea of getting an all-woman jury if possible.

After I saw the way things were going, I got Barney to one side.

"Play into his hands, Barney."

"What do you mean?"

"Let him get women on the jury."

"Gosh, no!" Quinn protested. "He's got too many of them on there now. Women go for him. He has a rich resonant voice. He looks soulfully into the eyes of each woman on the jury as he argues. He pays three hundred dollars for his suits, and he puts on a freshly pressed suit every morning. The guy's got enough property so he isn't dependent on his law practice. He wants adulation and influence. He's got his eye on being a state senator, attorney general and governor."

"Nevertheless," I said, "play into his hands. Let him get women on the jury."

Quinn sighed. "Hell," he said, "I don't know what we want a jury for anyway. The guy might as well plead guilty."

"What you need," I told him, "is a pint of liquor, a night's sleep and a babe. Get up on your toes. This case is either going to make you or break you."

"Well, it won't make me," he said gloomily. "*That's* for certain."

"Not if you go about it this way," I told him.

I stuck it through until court adjourned at five o'clock. Then I let Bertha drive her own car home. I rang up Stella Karis and made a dinner date.

We had cocktails, dinner and went back to her apartment for liqueurs. She didn't sit on the davenport. She sat in a chair. She was just a little reserved.

"How you coming with your boy friend?" I asked.

"What do you mean, my boy friend?"

"The banker."

"Oh, Cooper," she said. "You know, Donald, I'm afraid there's just a little jealousy on your part."

She looked at me archly.

"Perhaps there is," I admitted.

"Cooper is a good guy. He appeals to me a little teeny bit." She laughed throatily and said, "I don't know what appeals to *you*! You're one of the most stand-offish persons I've ever seen. I'll tell you one thing, Cooper's smart."

"I'm not stand-offish," I told her. "I'm working on this Endicott case and I'm worried about it."

"Why?"

"Confidentially," I said, "there's a witness I'm afraid the district attorney may uncover, a witness who can furnish motivation."

She lowered her lashes, looked at the tip of her cigarette. "Who is it?" she asked without looking at me.

"Girl by the name of Helen Manning," I said. "An ex-secretary. She worked for Endicott. Endicott fired her. It's not generally known, but she went to Mrs. Endicott and told her that Endicott was a heel, that he'd sent John Ansel into the Brazilian jungle so he could get him out of the way. It was a hell of a story."

"I can imagine how that must have made Mrs. Endicott feel," Stella said.

I didn't say anything. Stella Karis thought things over for a while. "You know, Donald," she said, "I think you're right at that. I think I should convert my property into securities that would give me an income and get back to my art work."

"Just be careful who holds the securities," I said.

She pursed her lips. "I can usually size up character," she said. "And if I can't, well, if anyone tries to give me a double cross, Donald, I'm ruthless, absolutely, utterly ruthless."

"Most women are," I told her, "but few admit it."

"I not only admit it, I'm proud of it. Don't ever try to give me a double cross, Donald."

"I won't," I said.

"I'm a hell cat," she said.

She got up to pour more liqueur. She was wearing some kind of a filmy white thing. The bottle was getting empty. She had another bottle in the kitchen. She opened the kitchen door to go get the bottle.

Bright lights were on in the kitchen. The lights flooded through the doorway and silhouetted every curve of her figure against the white gossamer.

Halfway through the doorway she thought of something, turned and said, "Would you prefer brandy and Benedictine to crème de menthe, Donald?"

91

I took a little time debating the matter. "You have both?" I asked.

"Yes." She shifted her position slightly.

The light behind her did its stuff.

"Brandy and Benedictine," I said. "But only a short one, Stella, I've got to go. I'm working on this damn case."

"You and your case!" she blazed.

"But when it's over," I said, "you're going to see more of me."

"By that time," she said angrily, "you may not be able to see *any* of *me*!"

She walked out into the kitchen, got the brandy and Benedictine. When she came back, she turned the kitchen lights out.

We had a brandy and Benedictine. I kissed her good night and went home.

At eight o'clock the next morning, my phone rang. I picked up the receiver and said hello.

The voice that replied was almost hysterical.

"Mr. Lam?"

"Yes."

"This is Helen, Helen Manning."

"Oh yes, Helen, what's on your mind?"

"I've just been served with a subpoena. There's an officer here. He says the district attorney of Orange County wants to talk with me."

"The officer's there now?" I asked.

"Yes."

"Where?"

"In the other room. I told him I had to go in the bedroom to change my clothes. What shall I do?"

"What can you do?" I asked.

She thought that over. "Nothing, I guess," she admitted.

"You could consult an attorney," I said. "But that wouldn't look so good. It would look as though you had something to conceal. You could refuse to talk, but that would simply centre attention on you. I guess about the only thing you *can* do is tell the truth."

"Oh, Mr. Lam. Donald, I wish I could talk with you."

"You can't," I told her. "I'm leaving right now for Santa Ana. I have to be in court while they're selecting a jury. You'd better tell them the truth."

"I can't. I simply *can't* tell them the truth."

"If you get caught in a mess of lies," I said, "it's going to look bad. There's one tip I can give you."

"What's that?" she asked.

"Mortimer Irvine, the district attorney of Orange County, is tall, dark, handsome, very impressionable and a bachelor. And in case you don't happen to know it, *you're* a dish!"

Her voice perked up. "Do *you* think so, Donald?"

"I know it," I said. "You have that something which radiates from a good-looking woman, personality, sex appeal, poise, the ability to wear clothes."

"Oh, Donald!"

"Don't talk with any of the deputies. Don't discuss anything with the officers. Say that your story is for the ears of the district attorney alone.

"You get it?" I went on. "*Alone.*"

Her voice showed a lot more vitality.

"Donald," she said, "you're wonderful! You're a tonic!"

"Be seeing you," I told her, and hung up.

CHAPTER NINETEEN

THINGS came to a showdown at eleven o'clock in the morning.

Judge Lawton said, "The peremptory is with the people."

Mortimer Irvine, on his feet, bowed from the waist, smiled at the court, turned soulful eyes to the jury. "The prosecution is entirely satisfied with the jury. The people waive the peremptory."

Judge Lawton looked at Barney Quinn.

Quinn half-swung around in his chair for a quick look at me. I gave him a quick signal of okay.

Quinn rose to his feet and to the occasion. He smiled a tired, baggy-eyed smile at the jurors, said, "If the Court please, the defendant in this case is entirely satisfied that this jury will give him the benefit of a fair and impartial trial."

Judge Lawton frowned a bit at the oratory, but said, "Very well. The jury will now be sworn to try the case. The other members of the venire, who are in attendance, will be excused. As soon as the jury is sworn, the Court will take a ten-minute recess, following which the district attorney will make his opening statement."

There was a considerable swirl of activity in the courtroom. Newspaper reporters pushed out of the doors, hurried to the telephones, to send a flash that the jury had been accepted and to give the names of the jurors.

Barney Quinn came over to stand beside me. After the first hubbub had subsided, he said, "Well, pretty quick we'll know the worst. We'll know what we're up against from his opening statement."

"Perhaps," I said. "On the other hand, if he has a surprise, he may deal in verbal detours."

"How am I doing?" Quinn asked.

"Better," I said. "Remember this. A jury keeps looking at the lawyers. The little things you do betray how you feel. The jurors don't pick it up from any one little thing you do but from the thousand little things you do. The way you tilt back in your chair. The way you look at the clock. The way you run your hand over your head. The way you get up when you address the court. The way you pick up a pencil. The speed with which you make notes. Everything registers.

"You can't sell a jury until you've first sold yourself. This is your big case. This is your opportunity. Make the most of it."

Quinn said gloomily, "This is Irvine's big case. It's also his big opportunity. This is where he launches his campaign for attorney general. He's smiling, urbane, persuasive—and, damn it! Lam, he's got eight women on the jury."

"So what?" I said. "What does he do when he gets mad? Does he blow up?"

"I don't know," Quinn said.

"That's a helluva way to practise criminal law," I told him. "Find out what he does when he gets mad."

Quinn gave me a wan smile. "I'm not usually this much of a washout, Lam, but this case has just taken the starch out of me. Tell me, did you find that gun?"

I looked him in the eyes. "No."

"You didn't?" he asked, his face lighting up.

"Hell, no!" I told him. "You're the attorney for the defence. I'd tell you the truth, wouldn't I? My God, man! We're working for you."

"You mean we're not suppressing any evidence?"

"Not a bit!"

He seemed to grow inches taller. "Well, why didn't you say so?"

"You didn't ask me."

"I was afraid to. I thought—Ansel was positive he'd thrown the gun into the hedge."

I said, "I doubt if he ever had a gun. You know what I think?"

"What?"

"I think the poor fool thinks that Elizabeth Endicott shot her husband, and he's half way trying to take the rap for her."

Quinn thought that over. "I'll be a sonofagun," he said slowly.

I saw the door of the Judge's chambers open. I gave Quinn a jab with my thumb. "Go on in there," I said, "and make the district attorney mad."

Judge Lawton called court to order. Mortimer Irvine started his opening statement in the well-modulated voice of a man who has taken a course in dramatics at college.

It was a statement of glittering generalities. He said he expected to prove that there had been an attachment between Elizabeth Endicott, the widow of Karl Carver Endicott, and the defendant John Dittmar Ansel. He expected to prove that, after Elizabeth Endicott consented to marry the decedent, Karl Endicott, the defendant Ansel had not been content to be a good loser, but had continued to hope against hope that he would be able to break up the home, notwithstanding the fact that he was in the employ of Karl Endicott, notwithstanding the fact that Endicott had trusted him to go on his most confidential missions. Ansel, as a snake in the grass, had waited, biding his time——

Barney Quinn was on his feet interrupting. He said he didn't want to interrupt but this was not the time for an argument. This was only an opening statement in which the district attorney was entitled to show what he expected to prove—not to engage in a lot of dramatics, not to try and impress his "soulful personality" on the jurors.

Judge Lawton got mad. Mortimer Irvine got mad. The judge rebuked Barney for the manner in which he had made his objection. The judge rebuked Irvine for abusing the privilege of the opening statement. Then the judge sustained the objection.

Irvine didn't do so good when he got mad. He lost some of his suave assurance. He had a savage, sarcastic streak in his character. The way I sized him up from that moment on he wasn't a fighter. When the going got tough he didn't wade in and slug. He circled around the edges and sniped.

Irvine went on. He said he expected to show that Ansel had returned from an expedition which he had voluntarily undertaken and for which he had received a bonus of twenty thousand dollars. He expected to show that within minutes of his arrival at the airport, Ansel had placed a telephone call. The telephone call had been to the residence of Karl Carver Endicott, but it had been a person-to-person call and the records would show that he had specifically stated he wished to talk only with Mrs. Endicott, and with no one else if she was not present.

Irvine went on to state that he expected to show Ansel had gone to the house. To the defendant's surprise the person who had answered the door had been Karl Carver Endicott. Endicott had invited the defendant to an upstairs room. Within a matter of minutes thereafter, Karl Carver Endicott had been dead, and Elizabeth Endicott had been a widow. Thereafter, Ansel had resorted to flight. He had remained in hiding, moving in the shadows, keeping from the clutches of the law only by reason of the fact that he was supposed to be dead. During that long waiting period, he had surreptitiously continued to meet Elizabeth Endicott.

Finally, when police had an inkling of the true facts, they had baited a trap and into that trap had walked the guilty pair—Elizabeth Endicott, the widow, who had been consorting with her husband's murderer even before the body of her husband was cold in death, and John Dittmar Ansel, the defendant in the case, who had repaid the opportunities for advancement Karl Carver Endicott had given him by a .38 bullet fired into the *back* of Endicott's head.

Irvine sat down amidst a hushed court-room. One or two of the younger feminine members of the jury looked at John Dittmar Ansel with revulsion stamped all over their faces.

Court took the noon recess.

"He's your baby," I told Barney Quinn. "He can't stand the

in-fighting. It musses up his good looks. Get in there and play-rough. Don't let him get away with that stuff about betraying the interests of his employer. Make an opening statement of your own right after court convenes. Tell the jurors that Endicott deliberately sent Ansel on a suicide trip, that he baited his trap with twenty thousand dollars, but was so ruthless he didn't even pay the twenty thousand in advance. It was only to be paid when the men returned, after having completed the impossible mission."

"But a defence lawyer shouldn't make his opening statement until he is ready to start putting on his case," Quinn said.

"Then you may not have any case to put on," I warned. "Right now you don't dare to put the defendant on the stand, and before you get done you probably won't dare to put Elizabeth Endicott on the stand. Tell them what you *expect* to prove, and pull out all the stops. Irvine talked about the loyalty due an employer from an employee. Tell them about the other side of the picture. Tell them about the man who sits smugly in an office and deliberately sends another man to his death, so that he can marry the man's sweetheart."

"The Court will rebuke me," Quinn said.

"The Court rebuked Irvine," I told him, "so you'll be even. Get started!"

Quinn did a pretty fair job at that. Irvine got mad. He was on his feet, waving his hands, interrupting.

As the story began to unfold from Quinn's lips, some of the women began to look sympathetically at John Ansel. Several of them glanced at Elizabeth Endicott and studied her poker face.

I made a note to remind Quinn to tell the jury that here was a woman who had suffered so much that she had abandoned tears as a useless expedient for emotional relief. Here was a woman who had had no outlet for her emotions for years, a woman who had suffered to the point of exhaustion.

Quinn began to get in his stride. He had more assurance and was showing some of the qualities that had given him a reputation as an up-and-coming trial lawyer.

By the time they started putting on evidence, most of the impression that Irvine had made on the jury with his opening argument had vanished. The jurors were interested and curious. They kept looking over the lawyers, the witnesses, the defendant, and above all Elizabeth Endicott.

After all, she was a public figure, the wealthy head of an oil empire, a mysterious woman who had kept to herself after the tragedy but who was now charged with having engaged in surreptitious meetings with a lover, a lover who in turn was hiding from the police.

The jurors prepared to enjoy all of the spicy details.

Irvine put on witnesses and went very briefly through the

necessary preliminaries: the fact of death, a surveyor who introduced a diagram of the premises, a photographer who showed photographs, an autopsy surgeon who had made a post-mortem examination showing that Karl Carver Endicott had been killed by a .38 calibre bullet, which had been fired into the *back* of his head, a bullet which had almost protruded from the forehead of the dead man.

The slug had been recovered and was introduced in evidence. The shot had been fired from such a distance that there were no powder burns. It was the opinion of the witness that the shot had been fired "a matter of feet" from the deceased at a time when the decedent had his back turned to the murderer.

Mortimer Irvine looked at the clock, then said dramatically, "Call Helen Manning to the stand."

Helen had dolled herself up. Aside from a few extra pounds, she was one good-looking babe and she knew it. You only needed one look at her as she got on the witness stand to know that the thing had worked in reverse. Instead of her dazzling Mortimer Irvine, *he* had turned loose *his* charm on her and had wrapped her around his finger.

She was like a well-trained dog on a leash doing exactly what was expected. She told her story in a low, throaty voice; that is, the story she wanted to tell.

She testified she had worked for Mr. Endicott for some years. She had finally decided to resign because the work was rather heavy for her, she wanted a change, and frankly there was a situation in the office that she didn't want to bother Mr. Endicott with, but which made it unpleasant for her. She was a highly competent secretary. She could get a position anywhere, and she chose to leave Mr. Endicott's employ. Mr. Endicott was very much concerned over her departure. He tried to find out what was wrong. He offered to make any adjustments that he could make, but she steadfastly refused to tell him why she was leaving because the young woman whom it was difficult for her to get along with was supporting a sick mother and needed the job. She wasn't a very good secretary anyway, and would have had difficulty getting other employment, whereas Helen was thoroughly competent, well trained and could go and get a job anywhere.

She had a letter signed by Mr. Endicott expressing his concern at losing her services, stating definitely that she was leaving of her own accord and recommending her very highly.

At about the time she was severing her connexion with the office, she had "been told" that the defendant John Dittmar Ansel had been sent into the Brazilian jungle on a suicide expedition. She had, unfortunately, believed this story and communicated it to Mrs. Endicott.

"And what did Mrs. Endicott say?" Irvine asked.

Quinn had his assurance back. He was on his feet with a roar. He accused the district attorney of misconduct. He objected to the question. He moved to strike out the entire evidence of the witness. Anything that had been communicated to Elizabeth Endicott was not evidence against the defendant and the district attorney knew it. This was an insidious attempt to prejudice the jury. It constituted prejudicial misconduct. Quinn assigned it as such, and asked the Court to disregard the statements of the witness and to admonish the district attorney.

Judge Lawton took rather a serious view of the matter. He called Irvine to account. "Just what is the position of the prosecution in this matter?" he said. "How do you contend that any communication made to Mrs Endicott is binding in any way upon the defendant?"

"We propose to show that Mrs. Endicott communicated what she had learned to the defendant," Ivine said.

"You are prepared to show that?"

"Well by inference," Irvine said.

Judge Lawton's face coloured. "Do you have first person evidence that will support that inference, Mr. Prosecutor?"

Irvine hedged. "Well, Your Honour, I think certain events speak for themselves. I think that the jurors should be permitted to draw an inference."

"I asked you a direct question," Judge Lawton interrupted. "Do you have first person, definite evidence which will give facts from which such an inference can be supported—as a matter of law now, not on a hope-so basis but on a legal basis?"

Irvine ran his hand around his collar. "I dislike to disclose my case in advance," he said. "If the Court will bear with me in this matter, I feel certain that it will be connected up."

"How?" Judge Lawton snapped.

"By circumstances and by the defendant's own admission," Irvine said.

Judge Lawton said, "It is up to the trial court to control the order of proof. I feel that this testimony could be highly prejudicial unless it is connected up. Before any more questions are asked of this witness, I suggest that you put on any evidence you may have showing how you propose to connect up this statement, how you propose to bring it home to the defendant."

"If the Court please, I'm not finished with this line of testimony," Irvine said.

"You're finished with it as far as this Court is concerned, and as far as this witness is concerned, until you show how you are going to connect it up," Judge Lawton said. "The Court controls the order of proof and the Court intends to protect the rights of the defendant in this matter. The Court feels that something is required other than the assurance of the prosecutor that the matter is going to be connected up."

"Very well," Irvine said. "May I withdraw this witness for a moment and put on another witness?"

"That witness is for the purpose of connecting up the testimony of this witness?"

"Yes, Your Honour."

"Very well," Judge Lawton said. "Now let's have no misunderstanding in the records as to what is happening. The motion is before the Court to strike the entire testimony of this witness from the record. A motion is before the Court to instruct the jury to disregard the questions and answers of this witness and to admonish the district attorney for prejudicial misconduct. The Court reserves the ruling upon all of those motions until the testimony of this next witness.

"You are at liberty to leave the witness stand temporarily, Miss Manning, but don't leave the court-room. Your testimony is not concluded. You are to be cross-examined upon your testimony. You are temporarily withdrawn so that the prosecutor may call his next witness.

"Now then, Mr. District Attorney, put on the witness by whom you hope to connect up this testimony with the defendant."

"Very well, Your Honour," Irvine said with poor grace. "Call John Small Ormsby."

Ormsby looked new all over. He had new shoes, a new ready-made suit, a new necktie and a new hair-cut. He looked a bit uncomfortable.

Ormsby, it turned out, was serving a sentence in the county jail. He had been convicted of having marijuana cigarettes in his possession. He had copped a plea and was serving a six months' sentence. He had ingratiated himself with the officers, had become a trusty, had been placed in the cell with John Dittmar Ansel, and had had a conversation with Ansel.

"What was the conversation?" Irvine asked.

Ormsby shifted his position on the witness stand, crossed his legs and the light glinted from his new shoes. "Well," he said, "it seems Ansel had just come back to his cell from a talk with his lawyer, and his lawyer had given him a rough time."

"Now just a minute," Judge Lawton interrupted. "We don't want you to testify to any of your conclusions. Just what was said?"

"Yes," Mr Irvine said unctuously, "what was said? Did Mr. Ansel *say* that his lawyer had given him a rough time?"

"Those were his exact words," Ormsby said. "He said his lawyer had given him a rough time."

"And what did he say after that?"

"He said that he'd broken down and told his lawyer about packin' a rod when he went out to call on Endicott that night.

He said he'd tossed the rod out of the window into the shrubbery
—into the hedge running along there."

"What else did he say?" Irvine asked.

"Well, he said he thought he'd made a mistake telling his
lawyer about that. He said it seemed to sort of take the starch
out of his lawyer."

The eyes of the jurors swivelled to Barney Quinn. Quinn had
the presence of mind to throw back his head and laugh silently.

"What else?" Irvine asked.

"Well, he said that Mrs. Endicott had told him about some
secretary who got sacked telling her all about how Endicott had
sent him——"

"Now, by him you are referring to Ansel?"

"That's right. Ansel said this secretary had told Mrs. Endicott all about how Endicott had deliberately sent him up the
Amazon so he could be put out of the way, and knowing that he
was going to get killed."

"Did he say anything else?"

"That was about all. He was going over it two or three times
with me. He asked me if I thought he'd made a mistake telling
his lawyer about the gun."

"Cross-examine," Irvine said to Quinn.

"He told you he'd thrown a gun out of the window?" Quinn
asked, smiling disdainfully.

"That's right."

"He said that was his gun?"

"Yes, sir, that's what he said."

"That he had taken it with him when he went to call on
Endicott?"

"Yes, sir."

"Did he say why he'd thrown it out of the window?"

"Well, he said he got a little sick to his stomach."

"What made him sick to his stomach? Did he say?"

"The thought of the girl he loved being married to a guy like
Endicott."

"Now then," Quinn said, pointing his finger at the witness,
"did he say he had fired the gun?"

"No, sir."

"Did he say that he hadn't fired the gun?"

"That's what he told me, that he hadn't fired it."

"Now then, did he tell you anything about *when* Mrs.
Endicott had told him about the secretary talking to her?"

"No, sir, he didn't."

"But you got the impression that it was long after the death
of Endicott that he was told about that, isn't that correct?"

"I object," Irvine said. "His impression is not important. The
question calls for a conclusion."

"Sustained," Judge Lawton said.

"Didn't he tell you that he hadn't seen Mrs. Endicott until after Endicott met his death?"

"Yes, sir, he did."

"So she couldn't have told him anything prior to that time?"

"Objected to as argumentative," Irvine said.

"Sustained," Judge Lawton said.

"But he did tell you definitely that, from the time he left for the jungles, he didn't see Mrs. Endicott until after Endicott's death?"

"Well, yes, he said that."

"Now you're a dope peddler, aren't you?" Quinn said.

"Objected to," Irvine said. "That is not a proper ground of impeachment. The witness can only be impeached by showing that he has been convicted of a felony."

"This question may, however, be preliminary. It may go to the question of bias," Judge Lawton said.

"Then the other question should be asked first," Irvine said.

"Very well, I'll sustain the objection at this time."

"You are in jail as a prisoner?" Quinn said.

"Yes, sir."

"And how long have you been in jail?"

"A little over four months."

"And how long do you still have to serve?"

"About ten days, figuring good time."

"And why were you sent to jail?"

"I had marijuana cigarettes in my possession."

"Were you smoking them?"

"Yes, sir."

"Were you peddling them?"

"Objected to as incompetent, irrelevent and immaterial, and not proper cross-examination," Irvine said.

"Sustained," Judge Lawton ruled.

"Didn't you have a conversation with the officers, the substance of which was that while the officers *could* charge you with peddling marijuana cigarettes, if you would give your testimony in this case, they would not press that charge against you?"

"Well . . . no."

"Didn't you have a conversation with some of the officers to the effect that if you would move into the cell with the defendant John Dittmar Ansel, and try to inveigle him into conversation so that you could get some admission from him that could be used as testimony, you'd be released from jail and not be prosecuted on a charge of dope peddling?"

"No, sir, not in those words."

Quinn looked scornfully at the witness.

"How long have you had those shoes?" Quinn asked, pointing disdainfully at the shoes.

"I got 'em yesterday."

"Where did you get them?"

"In a shoe store."

"You're supposed to be in jail. How did you get out of jail?"

"The sheriff let me out."

"Where did you get those pants?"

"In a clothing store."

"When?"

"Yesterday."

"Where did you get that coat?"

"In a clothing store."

"When?"

"Yesterday."

"Who paid for the suit?"

"The sheriff."

"Who paid for the shoes?"

"The sheriff."

"When was your hair cut last?"

"Yesterday."

"Who paid for the haircut?"

"The sheriff."

"Where was your hair cut?"

"At a barber shop uptown."

"Don't you know they have barbers in the jail?"

"I don't know."

"How long have you been there?"

"Four and a half months."

"You've had your hair cut in that time, haven't you?"

"Yes, sir."

"By whom?"

"By a barber in the jail."

"But yesterday, after you had run to the officers with this story, after you had played stool pigeon for them, a jail haircut wasn't good enough for you. In order to impress this jury, the officers took you up to a high-class barber and gave you the works, didn't they?"

"Well, they took me uptown."

"That's a new necktie you have on, isn't it?"

"Yes."

"Who paid for that?"

"The sheriff."

Barney Quinn turned from the man in disgust.

"That's all," he said.

"No further questions," Irvine said.

The witness left the stand.

"Now then, Your Honour," Quinn said, "I renew my motion to strike out the entire testimony of the witness Helen Manning

103

because it becomes apparent that anything she told Mrs. Endi-cott could not possibly have been communicated to the defend-ant prior to the death of the decedent. I renew my motion that the district attorney be admonished for misconduct, and that the jury be instructed to disregard everything that the district attorney said and everything that the witness Helen Manning said on the stand."

Judge Lawton leaned forward on the bench, weighed his words carefully. "The motion to strike the testimony of Helen Manning will be granted. The jury is instructed to pay no atten-tion whatever to the testimony of this witness. The effect will be as though this witness had never been called to the stand.

"The Court recognizes the assignment of misconduct on the part of the district attorney to this extent. The jurors are instructed to pay no attention to any remarks made by the district attorney or to any statements made by counsel on either side except insofar as those statements are substantiated by evidence that is permitted to go before the jury. The Court instructs the jurors to completely disregard all statements made by the district attorney in connexion with the testimony of the witness Manning to the effect that he would connect up the testimony.

"Now then, Mr. Prosecutor, proceed with your next wit-ness."

"My next witness, if the Court please," Irvine said, "is one who will still further connect up the testimony that——"

"That testimony has been stricken," Judge Lawton rebuked. "You may move to have it reinstated if at any time you can connect it up. The Court feels that the proof was put on out of order. The Court feels that the prosecutor should have put on any evidence he might have had seeking to connect up the testimony of the witness Manning before putting the witness Manning on the stand.

"The Court feels that any further reference on the part of the prosecution to testimony which has been stricken from the record may well constitute prejudicial misconduct. Now, pro-ceed."

"Very well," Irvine said, with poor grace, "call Steven Beardsley."

Beardsley, a tall, gangling individual, came to the stand and was sworn.

"What's your occupation, Mr. Beardsley?"

"I'm deputy sheriff in this county."

"Is there any particular field in which you have specialized, any field in the nature of law enforcement?"

"Yes, sir."

"What is that field?"

"Ballistics. Firearms identification."

"Will you tell us what training you have had along these lines?"

"I have studied under several of the leading men in the country. I have been making a practice of firearms identification for more than ten years."

"Are you familiar with the town of Citrus Grove in this county?"

"I am, yes, sir."

"Are you familiar with the premises known as the Whippoorwill, the estate of Karl Carver Endicott?"

"I am, yes, sir."

"Do you recognize the premises shown on this map, People's Exhibit No. One?"

"I do, yes, sir."

"I will ask you if you have at any time searched the hedge shown on People's Exhibit No. One?"

"I have, yes, sir."

"I will ask you if at any time within the past week you found a weapon in that hedge?"

"I did, yes, sir."

"Do you have that weapon with you?"

"I do."

"Produce it please."

The witness produced a rust-encrusted, blued-steel revolver.

"What is that?"

"That is a Colt .38 calibre revolver."

"How many shells are in that revolver?"

"Five shells with bullets in them and one empty chamber in the cylinder."

"Have you been able to fire test bullets through that gun?"

"I have had considerable difficulty restoring it to a condition where it is safe to fire it, but I have removed enough of the rust to enable the mechanism to function. I had purposely refrained from removing any of the rust which was not essential for this purpose in order to show the condition of the weapon when it was found."

"From your test have you been able to determine whether that was the weapon from which the bullet was fired which killed Karl Carver Endicott?"

"Well, I'll put it this way. The barrel has been badly rusted. The individual markings from that barrel are such that it is impossible to make an identification. All I can state is that this revolver is a .38 Colt revolver firing bullets of a certain type and the bullet which was taken from the head of Mr. Endicott is the same calibre as the bullet which was taken from this revolver, has the same characteristics, and both bullets were fired from a .38 calibre Colt revolver."

"In other words, there is no reason from the standpoint of

ballistic science why the bullet which was taken from the head of Karl Carver Endicott could *not* have been fired from this revolver?"

"That is right. This revolver could have fired the fatal bullet."

"Have you traced the ownership of that revolver so that you know whose revolver it is?"

"I have, yes, sir."

"Whose is it?"

"Objected to as not the best evidence, as calling for hearsay evidence, as calling for a conclusion of the witness and invading the province of the jury," Barney Quinn said.

Irvine seemed annoyed. "If the Court please, we can get at this another way, but it is going to be a costly procedure and will necessitate the calling of a witness who will have to take a plane to be here."

"Nevertheless," Judge Lawton ruled, "that is one of the constitutional guarantees of a man charged with crime. He has the right to be faced with the witnesses against him and to have the privilege of cross-examining them. I take it this witness now on the stand doesn't know of his own knowledge to whom the weapon belongs, only that he has conducted investigations as an officer which have convinced him that the weapon is the property of a certain person."

"That is right, Your Honour."

"The objection is sustained," Judge Lawton said. "It now appears that we have reached the hour of the afternoon adjournment. Court will take a recess until tomorrow morning. In the meantime, the defendant is remanded to the custody of the sheriff and the jurors are admonished not to discuss the case among yourselves not to permit anyone to discuss it in your presence. You are not to form or express any opinion until the case is finally submitted to you for a decision.

"Court will recess until tomorrow morning at ten o'clock."

Quinn walked past me on his way out of the court-room. "Meet me in my office," he said in an undertone.

I fell into step beside him. "What do you want?"

"To discuss the evidence."

"To hell with it!" I told him. "I've got something else to do. Keep on the end of your telephone so I can reach you at any hour of the night. Get what sleep you can. This is going to be one hell of a night!"

I beckoned to Bertha, and we pushed our way through the crowd.

"Now what?" Bertha asked.

"Now," I said, "we go to our own ballistics expert in Pasadena and find out what the hell *we* dug up in the garden."

"It's a .38 calibre Colt revolver," Bertha said.

106

"Probably the murder weapon. That means one of us has got to be called as a witness."

"Oh, my God!" Bertha said.

We drove to Pasadena where one of the best legal physicists in the country has his office. We started him working on the gun. Within half an hour he had the number of the gun, and within another hour we had the answer.

The gun had been purchased by Helen Manning six years ago.

I hung up the phone and turned to Bertha. "This," I said, "is going to be in your province, Bertha. You're going to have to take a babe apart."

"Who?"

"Helen Manning."

"That bitch!" Bertha said.

"Can you take her apart?"

"*I'll* take her apart," Bertha promised. "I'll have her sawdust stuffing spilled all over the floor of her apartment."

"Let's go," I told her.

CHAPTER TWENTY

I PRESSED the buzzer on Helen Manning's apartment.

"Who is it?" she called through the doorway in dulcet tones.

"Donald Lam," I said.

"Just a minute, Donald."

She waited a moment, then laughed and said, "I was just in the shower. Let me put something on."

Bertha and I waited for about five minutes; then the door opened.

The clothes she had put on were fluffy, semi-transparent and good-looking. She raised her eyes to mine and said demurely, "You'll have to pardon my appearance, Donald, I just came out of the bath and—— Who's this?"

Bertha Cool barged on into the room like a fortified tank moving in on an enemy front line of entrenchments.

"I'm Bertha Cool," she said. "I'm a detective. Cut out the lollygagging and get the hell down to business.

"Sit down there where I can look at you."

Bertha kicked the door shut with her heel.

"What the hell was the idea of shooting Karl Endicott?" she demanded.

Helen Manning fell back. Her hand went to her throat; her eyes were wide. "What in the world are you talking about?"

"*You* know what I'm talking about," Bertha said. "You went down to see Endicott the day he was killed. You took your gun with you, didn't you, dearie?

"When you were so nasty nice on the witness stand today, when you were billing and cooing with that romantic-looking district attorney down there, you didn't tell him the whole story. You didn't tell him about having bought a gun did you?"

"Well, *I'll* tell you all about that gun, dearie. You bought that gun down at a sporting goods store in Santa Ana, and it was a nice little .38 calibre Colt revolver. You bought it two days before Karl Endicott was murdered. You haven't had it in your possession since Karl Endicott was murdered.

"Now, won't *that* be nice to tell the district attorney?"

Helen Manning said, "Why you ... I didn't ... I never——"

"Don't tell me you didn't," Bertha screamed at her. "You're not showing your goddam legs to some impressionable man now. You're talking to a woman who knows *all* the tricks. And don't pull that business of being a little lady with me. You were sleeping with Karl Endicott and you didn't mind his getting married as long as you were the number one mistress, but when he ran somebody else in and relegated you to number two position you went off your trolley."

"I . . . I——" Helen Manning started to sob.

"That's right, go ahead and bawl," Bertha said. "Keeps you from having to look in my eyes. But it isn't going to do you any good. When you get your tears all dried up you're going to be facing Bertha Cool, not Donald Lam. Now cut out the water-works and give me the low-down before I decide to *really* get tough."

"What . . . what do you want?"

"What happened the night Endicott was murdered?"

"I . . . I don't know."

"The hell you don't," Bertha said. "You told Mrs. Endicott all about Karl sending John Ansel up into the Amazon on a trip from which he wasn't supposed to return. You really spilled your guts there. And she had to go and spill the story to her husband. That put the fat in the fire and the husband tele-phoned for you. That's my best guess. Anyway you were there the night he was murdered. You were there when John Ansel came in. You were the girl who was in the upstairs bedroom. And after you killed him, you thought your gun would never be found. Well, dearie, for your information, we found your gun and the ballistics expert will testify that the fatal bullet was fired from that gun, a gun you bought two days before in a sporting goods store in Santa Ana. Now do you want to talk or do you want me to get the police up here and have the newspaper reporters rip your life wide open?"

Bertha stood over Helen Manning, glaring down at her, and Bertha was hard. There was no mistake about that. When Bertha got hard, she got hard.

Helen Manning said, "I didn't shoot him, Mrs. Cool, I honestly didn't."

"Who did?"

"Cooper Hale was the only one who *could* have done it."

"Now you're talking," Bertha Cool said. "Let's get some facts in the case. What happened?"

She said, "I told his wife. His wife told him about what I had said. He was furious. He sent for me to come down to see him. I was frightened. I had bought that gun——

"I don't know what I intended to do, but . . . I had been very fond of Karl Endicott and . . . I had given him much more than he had given me. I had given him my heart. I had given him the best years of my life. I——"

"Can that stuff!" Bertha said. "Give me the facts. We haven't got much time!"

She said, "When I arrived there at the house, he told me that Mr. Hale was coming at almost any minute. He took me to an upstairs room, a bedroom. He was nice to me. He said his wife had left him. He ... he was awfully nice. He took me in his arms and ... well, his hands ... he found the gun."

"And then what?"

"He laughed and took it away from me and put it on the dresser.

"And then the doorbell rang. That was Hale.

"He told me to wait. He said that he was coming back, that Hale wouldn't be there very long.

"I was so confused and upset and I just didn't know what to do. And then the doorbell rang again. That was John Ansel. I thought John Ansel was dead. It startled me to hear his voice. Karl took Ansel upstairs and excused himself for a minute. He came into the bedroom and said, in a whisper, 'You'll have to beat it, darling, the situation has become too complicated. Get back to town and I'll call you later on.' Then he gave me a little pat and a kiss and said, 'Go on downstairs quietly and fade out of the picture.' "

"All right, what did you do?"

"I went down the stairs. As I reached the sidewalk I heard a revolver shot from the upstairs bedroom."

"What did you do?" Bertha Cool asked.

"I hesitated a moment, and then I ran. I ran to the corner and then walked and walked and walked until it seemed I couldn't walk another step, and finally I caught a bus back to the city.

"I knew ... deep down in my heart ... I knew what had happened. I knew he was dead."

Bertha looked at me.

"Write it down," I said.

We moved her over to a table and gave her paper. She wrote it down.

"Sign it!" I said.

She signed it.

"Date it!" I said.

She dated it.

Bertha Cool and I signed as witnesses.

I said, "Did you realize you were sending an innocent man to the gas chamber?"

"I didn't know what to do," she said. "I tried to keep out of it. But you don't understand what it means to me, Donald. My whole career ... I have a good job. I'm a very competent secretary and in this job I'm working up. I'm getting a good salary. The faintest breath of scandal and I'd be out, and ... and I'm not young any more. That is, I'm——"

"What the hell are you talking about?" Bertha said. "Don't tell me you're not young. Why you're only about thirty-five. That's just the right age for a woman to begin living. You know what it's all about. You know how men think and you know how they work, and if you're any good at all you know how to drive 'em nuts.

"You make me sick with that all-washed-up line. And don't ever hand out any more of that best-years-of-your-life crap. That's the thing that chases men away faster than a smallpox quarantine sign. Quit eating so goddam many sweets, and set your cap for some of these guys. You're just entering on the best years of your life right now."

"I know," Helen said dolefully, "but the men I know are already married, nearly all of them."

"Ain't that too bad!" Bertha Cool said unsympathetically. "I don't see any signs of frustration about you, dearie." She walked over to a chair, picked up a girdle, looked at it a minute, threw it in a corner and said, "The way you're built, it's a goddam shame to strap yourself into one of those things. Cut out a few calories and get that bottom of yours back into circulation.

"Come on, Donald."

We left Helen Manning sobbing.

"Well?" Bertha Cool said.

"Go to bed," I told her. "I'm taking this thing down to Barney Quinn."

"Well, let's hope it cheers him up," Bertha said.

"Having a client lie to you is a devastating experience, particularly when you prepare your entire defence on a false assumption," I told her.

"I know," Bertha said. "How did I do in there? Was I hard enough?"

"You were hard enough."

"It serves her right," Bertha said, "for not feathering her nest. She should have done some gold digging on the sonofabitch and then she'd have had enough money so she wouldn't need to work when the bust-up came."

"How did she know there was going to be a bust-up?" I asked.

"Phooey!" Bertha said. "With a guy like this Karl Endicott there's always a bust-up. Can you imagine that goddam blonde thinking she's all done at thirty-five. Hell! She's just starting! Five pounds off her bottom and she's ready for the races. Thirty-five is just the right age. She's begun to find out what it's all about by that time. All right, Donald, you get on down to see Barney Quinn. Bertha's going out and have herself a great, big, juicy steak. Thank God, *I* don't have to worry about *my* fat bottom. I'm finished with men."

CHAPTER TWENTY-ONE

BARNEY QUINN was pacing the floor of his office.

"I'm beginning to think we can make it, Donald," he said. "It's a good jury, and I think we've aroused their sympathy."

"All right," I told him. "Here's what you do. Tomorrow Irvine finishes with the ballistics expert. On the strength of finding Ansel's gun in the hedge, he tries again to bring in the testimony of Helen Manning."

Quinn laughed. "*That* won't get him any place. Judge Lawton has kicked her testimony out of court, and he's going to——"

"Hold everything!" I told him. "When Irvine moves to reinstate the evidence of Helen Manning on account of the corroboration furnished by finding the gun, you tell the Court that, under the circumstances, Irvine's point appears to be well taken and you're withdrawing your motion to strike Helen Manning's testimony from the record."

"What?" Barney exclaimed incredulously. "Are you crazy?"

"Then," I said, "Irvine walks into the trap. He goes ahead and puts on the rest of his case consisting of Nickerson and Cooper Hale. Hale will tell a convincing story. Then the district attorney will rest and throw the case in your lap.

"At that time you call the attention of the Court to the fact that Helen Manning was withdrawn from the stand and you have never had a chance to cross-examine her."

Barney Quinn said, "That would be sheer suicide."

"And," I went on, "You get Helen Manning back on the stand for cross-examination. Then you lower the boom on the district attorney."

"What do you mean, lower the boom?"

I tossed the signed statement on his desk.

Barney Quinn sat down to read the statement. He read the first few lines, then suddenly snapped bolt upright in his chair. His eyes raced through the rest of the statement down to the signature and the date. He looked at me with awed admiration, got up and shook hands. Then he went to a bookcase, swung back the false bindings of half a dozen books, disclosed a liquor closet, took out a bottle and two glasses.

"Not for me," I said, "I'm driving a car."

Barney Quinn held the neck of the bottle over the glass until the gurgling sounds changed from the low-pitched *gloog-gloog* to a high-pitched *cluck-cluck-cluck*.

"Go ahead and drive back," he said. "I've got a load off my mind and I'm going to get the first good night's sleep I've had since I started this damn case. Boy, oh boy! What a smear! Wait till I see Irvine's face when he walks into this one."

"Now wait a minute," I cautioned him. "Don't be too damn sure. That boy Irvine is smart, and this Manning girl is keenly aware of his soulful eyes, his wide shoulders and his slim hips."

Quinn picked up the signed statement. "Let me slap her in the face with that, and I don't give a damn if she's sleeping with the guy."

I said, "Then you'd better get finished by tomorrow or she will be."

He raised the glass and tossed off about half of the big drink of whisky. A slow smile suffused his features.

"Damn, but that feels good!" he said.

CHAPTER TWENTY-TWO

THE morning session opened with Irvine calling a witness from New Orleans. The witness testified that he operated a store there, that he had sold the revolver introduced in evidence on behalf of the prosecution to the defendant John Dittmar Ansel some years earlier. He produced a firearms register bearing the signature of the defendant, and he identified the defendant.

There was no cross-examination.

"Now then, if the Court please," Irvine said as a matter of routine, the tone of his voice showing that his spirit wasn't in it, "I would like to move again to reinstate the evidence of the witness Manning."

Judge Lawton had opened his mouth to deny the motion when Barney Quinn was on his feet.

"May I be heard, Your Honour?"

"It won't be necessary," Judge Lawton said.

"Very well, Your Honour, thank you, Your Honour. The defendant feels that, with the identification of the firearm in question, the testimony of the witness Manning has been connected up and the defendant withdraws his motion to strike the evidence of the witness."

"You do *what*?"

"We withdraw our motion to strike out the evidence. The defendant believes that technically the evidence should now be permitted to stand."

"Well, the Court doesn't feel that way," Judge Lawton snapped.

Irvine was quick to grab at the advantage. "The defendant has withdrawn his objection, withdrawn his motion to strike out the testimony of the witness Manning?"

"That is correct," Quinn said.

Judge Lawton hesitated a long while.

"Under those circumstances," Irvine said, "it would seem there is no question before the Court, and the testimony of this witness is reinstated."

"Very well," Judge Lawton said, and frowned at Quinn.

Thereafter, Drude Nickerson was called to the stand.

Nickerson, a paunchy, ward-heeler type, went back in his testimony to the time when he had been driving a taxicab on the night of the shooting. He identified Ansel as the man whom he had picked up at the airport sometime after eight in the evening, the man who had been nervous and upset, the man whom he had driven to the residence of Karl Carver Endicott.

114

Quinn made only a perfunctory cross-examination of Nickerson.

The district attorney then called Cooper Franklin Hale to the stand

Hale walked quietly to the stand, took the oath, gave his name and address, and eased himself cautiously into the witness chair, as though making certain there were no hidden wires or secret traps.

Hale testified that he had gone out to Endicott's house the night of the shooting, that Endicott had received a visitor, had excused himself and had gone upstairs, that Hale had waited downstairs for Endicott to finish his business with the man who had interrupted the session by ringing the doorbell, that he had heard a revolver shot from upstairs, that he had started for the stairs and had seen the figure of a man dashing downstairs immediately after the shot had been fired. He identified the man as being the defendant John Dittmar Ansel.

Again Quinn asked a few questions.

"That's the prosecution's case, Your Honour," Irvine said.

"If the Court please," Quinn said, getting to his feet, "we were not given the opportunity to cross-examine the witness Manning. It was understood that she was withdrawn from the stand, and——"

"Her testimony was stricken out," Irvine said, "and subsequently reinstated without any motion on the part of the defence for the right to cross-examine."

"That makes no difference," Judge Lawton ruled. "The understanding was the defendant was to have an opportunity to cross-examine this witness. The Court lost sight of that matter because the Court felt that—— Never mind. The witness Manning will return to the stand for cross-examination."

Helen had really prepared for the newspaper photographers.

Barney Quinn started in on her gently.

Wasn't it true that she had told Mrs. Endicott about John Ansel being sent on a suicide expedition some two days before Karl Endicott met his death?

The witness admitted that it was true.

"Now isn't it a fact," Quinn went on, "that Karl Endicott telephoned you on the day of his death and told you that you had made an assertion to his wife that was false, that he desired an opportunity to explain his side of the matter to you, that he was very much concerned that you had taken office gossip as your source of information and had not given him a chance to explain?"

"Yes."

"And didn't you go out to his house at his request on the date of his death?"

"Yes."

"And," Quinn shouted, getting to his feet and levelling his finger at her, "didn't you carry a .38 calibre Colt revolver in your purse that night?"

"It wasn't in my purse. It was in my bra."

"There is no reason to shout at the witness," Irvine said in a low voice. "There is no call for all of these dramatics."

Judge Lawton seemed completely bewildered. He looked from the suave district attorney to the attorney for the defence and then to the witness on the stand. "Proceed," he said.

"And isn't it a fact that, when you went out there that evening, the decedent, Karl Carver Endicott, your former employer, told you that he was expecting a visitor in the person of Cooper Franklin Hale, and didn't he ask you to go upstairs and wait up there until after he had been able to get rid of Mr. Hale?"

"Yes."

"And you went upstairs with him?"

"Yes."

"Into a bedroom?"

"Yes."

"And there Mr. Endicott discovered the weapon that you had in your possession?"

"Yes."

"And what did he do with it?"

"He removed the weapon and chided me for carrying it."

"And then what happened?"

"Then there was a ring at the doorbell, and Mr. Endicott told me that that was Mr. Hale and I would have to excuse him."

"And then what?"

"Then he went downstairs and was down there for some fifteen minutes when the bell again rang and Mr. Endicott met the defendant at the front door."

"Do you know it was the defendant?"

"I heard his voice."

"You knew the defendant?"

"Yes."

"You knew his voice?"

"Yes."

"And what did Mr. Endicott do?"

"Took Mr. Ansel . . . I mean the defendant upstairs and into the den."

"And this den adjoined the bedroom where you were waiting?"

"Yes."

"And then what happened?"

"Mr. Endicott excused himself and entered the bedroom and told me that the situation had become more complicated than he had anticipated and that I had better go home, but that he would get in touch with me later on and arrange for a meeting."

"And what did you do?" Quinn asked, his manner showing his complete surprise at what was happening.

Here was a witness who should have been hysterical, who should have been in tears, who should have been reluctantly making damaging admissions, and she was sitting in the witness stand, cool, calm, and collected, answering his questions without the slightest embarrassment. Here was the district attorney, who should have been bordering on panic as he saw his carefully constructed case being shattered to smithereens, and Irvine was standing cool, suave, and sardonic, his manner that of one who is patiently putting up with tactics of a minor pettifogging nature simply because he doesn't want to waste the time of the Court with objections.

A deputy sheriff tiptoed along the aisle of the court-room and put a folded piece of paper into my hand. It was a message from our expert in Pasadena. It stated that he had been served with a *subpoena duces tecum* to appear and bring the gun with him into court.

I knew then we were sunk. I frantically tried to catch Quinn's eye before he asked the one last fatal question.

"What did you do after that?"

She said, "I left the house and left the gun lying there on the bureau in the bedroom."

"Who was in the bedroom?"

"The decedant, Karl Endicott."

"And where was the defendant?"

"In the adjoining den."

Quinn said, "That's all," and sat down. He was like a man who had hurled his weight against a door to smash it open, and found the door unlocked and unlatched.

District Attorney Irvine smiled benignly. "That is all, Miss Manning. And thank you very much for your frank statement of the facts."

The witness started to leave the stand.

"Oh, just a moment," Irvine said. "I have one question, and only one question, Miss Manning. Did you make a statement of what you have just testified to the defence in this case?"

"Yes."

"When?"

"Last night."

"To whom was that statement made?"

"To two detectives employed by the defendant, Donald Lam and Bertha Cool."

"Thank you, thank you. That is all," Irvine said.

The witness left the stand.

Irvine said, "Now, Your Honour, in view of the testimony of this witness, it becomes necessary for me to call one more witness."

He called our expert from Pasadena.

The expert identified the gun as having been received from us. He had, he admitted, cleaned up the gun so that he could fire a test bullet through it. He had not had access to the fatal bullet, and, therefore, he could not state whether that was the gun from which the fatal bullet had been fired.

"If you were given an opportunity to consult with the prosecution's expert and an opportunity to examine the fatal bullet, do you feel that you can reach such a conclusion?" Irvine asked.

The expert said he thought he could.

The smiling Irvine suggested that the witness leave the stand and be given an opportunity to make such an examination, that Steven Beardsley, the ballistics expert for the prosecution, would be only too glad to co-operate in every way with an expert of such renowned professional standing.

And then Irvine asked to recall Cooper Hale to the stand briefly. That did it.

Cooper Hale testified that, after hearing the shot, he had dashed upstairs, that he had found Endicott lying dead on the floor, that there was a bullet hole in the back of his head, that there *was no gun on the bureau in the room.*

"Now then," Irvine said, "let me ask you a few questions about more recent events, Mr. Hale. Where do you live at the present time?"

Hale gave his his address.

"And where is that with reference to the estate known as the Whippoorwill, the estate of Karl Carver Endicott, deceased?"

"It is next door."

"In the adjoining house?"

"Yes."

"Directing your attention to the night before the commencement of this trial, did you notice anything unusual taking place at that time in the Endicott residence?"

"Yes, sir."

"What?"

"Two persons were digging something up in a hedge of the Endicott home."

"Did you have an opportunity to see those persons or recognize them?"

"Yes. I recognized them by their voices."

"Will you tell us what happened?"

"My house was dark. I had retired. It was well after midnight. I saw two individuals vaguely out in the hedge. I was curious, so I put on a dark robe and slipped out a side door. I learned from their low-voiced conversation that they were digging something up."

"And then what happened?"

"I heard one of them say, 'I found it!'"

"Do you know who that person was?"

"Yes, sir."

"Who?"

"Donald Lam, a detective employed by the defence."

"Had you heard his voice before?"

"Yes."

"You recognized that voice?"

"I did."

"Now then, prior to that time had you seen anyone *burying* anything near the location of the hedge?"

"Yes, sir."

"Who?"

"Mrs. Endicott."

"You mean Elizabeth Endicott, the widow of Karl Carver Endicott?"

"Yes, sir."

"What had you seen her burying?"

"I don't know what it was. It was something she took from a package. She dug a little hole in the ground, and placed this thing, whatever it was, in that hole, and covered it loosely with earth."

"When was that?"

"It was the same night."

"What time?"

"About an hour before Mr. Lam and Mrs. Cool dug up the gun."

"Did you hear them refer to it as a gun?"

"Yes."

"Now with reference to the place you saw this thing being buried, where was that? At what particular spot in the hedge? Can you point it out on the map?"

The witness pointed to a spot on the map.

"Now mark that with an 'X' and put your initials near it."

The witness did so.

"With reference to the place where you saw this gun being dug up, or rather where you heard the persons at work digging up the weapon, can you identify that?"

"Yes, sir."

"Where was it?"

"At exactly the same place, as nearly as I can tell," the witness said.

Irvine turned to Quinn with a smile. "Cross-examine," he said.

Fortunately at that point Quinn had sense enough to direct the Court's attention to the fact that it was time for the mid-morning recess.

The Court took its recess and Quinn came over to me.

"It's all right," I told him. "We're going to out-smart them yet."

"But what the hell happened?"

"What happened," I said, "is perfectly obvious. That damn district attorney, with his romantic bearing, his expressive eyes, has completely hypnotized Helen Manning. She's eating out of his hand. He's convinced her that he's her dish. She must have telephoned him as soon as we left her apartment and told him what had happened.

"There wasn't, of course, any way that we could have prevented that. If we'd been the prosecution, we could have taken her into custody so she couldn't have communicated with the other side.

"So the district attorney gets hold of Hale and tells him the sad news and Hale laughs, says he was just waiting for us to walk into that trap and tells the prosecutor for the first time about having seen Mrs. Endicott burying something in the hedge and about seeing us digging something up."

"Do you think Irvine would let him do that without asking him why he hadn't told his story before?"

"He asked all right, and Hale undoubtedly explained that he thought the authorities had the murder weapon, that he didn't know exactly what we had found and that he was waiting to see what sort of a frame-up we were cooking up before showing *his* hand."

"Irvine isn't that dumb," Quinn said. "Hale is lying."

"We can't prove it, and Irvine is so damned sold on his side of the case that it colours his judgement in everything he does. He wants to win this case."

"But what are we going to do now?" Quinn asked.

I said, "This is where you tear into that witness Hale. You ask him if it isn't a fact that he came to my office and offered to shade his testimony so the defendant would be acquitted if we'd give him the breaks on leasing some of his property to an eastern manufacturer."

"What?" Quinn exclaimed, startled. "You mean he made a proposition like that?"

"Ask him."

"But I couldn't ask him unless I had your assurance that such was the case."

"Ask him," I said. "You're going to have to fight the devil with fire."

"Will you assure me that you'll get on the stand and testify that he said that?"

"No," I said, "I won't get on the stand and testify he said that in so many words. However, that was what he had in mind and he won't be able to remember exactly what he said. Go ahead and ask him that."

120

"Not unless you tell me that you'll testify to that effect."

I said, "Ask him why he went to our office. Ask him if he didn't go there and suggest that he was a personal friend of the district attorney and that he would try to intercede on behalf of the defendant if I would co-operate with him."

"Will you testify to that?"

"I'll go this far, such an offer was made in his presence and with his approval."

Court reconvened. Hale, smilingly self-confident, waited for the cross-examination.

Quinn said, "Isn't it a fact that you have been acquainted with Donald Lam and Bertha Cool, the two detectives, for some time?"

"Not for a long time. For a relatively short time."

"Isn't it a fact that you told Mr. Lam and his partner Mrs. Cool that you were a friend of the district attorney?"

"I may have. I consider the district attorney my friend. I know many of the officials of this county and consider them my friends."

"Didn't you offer to intercede on behalf of the defendant with the district attorney if Mr. Lam would co-operate with you in a private business matter?"

"I did not."

"Didn't you offer to use your good offices with the district attorney in trying to make things easier for the defendant in this case, if Cool and Lam would work with you in a certain property matter? And didn't they refuse to do so and thereby cause you to make threats?"

"Definitely not!"

"Didn't that conversation take place in their office?"

"No, sir."

"Were you ever in their office?"

The witness hesitated.

"Were you?" thundered Quinn.

"Well, yes."

"Before the trial of this case?"

"Yes."

"After the defendant had been arrested?"

"I believe it was. I can't remember the exact date."

"Didn't you discuss this case with Mr. Lam and Mrs. Cool at that time?"

"We discussed a number of things."

"Answer that question! Didn't you discuss this case with them?"

"I may have mentioned it."

"And in that connexion, didn't you discuss your friendship with the district attorney?"

"I may have."

"Didn't you suggest that you would be willing to co-operate?"

"Co-operate is a very loose word, Mr. Quinn."

"I understand the meaning of the English language," Quinn said. "Didn't you offer to co-operate?"

"I may have used the word. But what I meant by it may have been entirely different from what the other parties *thought* I meant by it."

"But you did go to their office?"

"Yes."

"After the case was pending?"

"Yes."

"And you did mention your friendship for the district attorney?"

"Yes. Either I did or my companion did."

"And you did offer to use your good offices in case they would co-operate?"

"Well, I may have, or I may have offered something in the nature of co-operation. I don't know."

"All right. Wasn't that offer refused?"

"There wasn't any definite offer which could have been refused."

"You left the office after making some threats?"

"I—— No."

"Would you say you left the office with the same friendly, good feeling with which you had entered it?"

"Yes."

"Did you shake hands with Donald Lam when you left?"

"I can't remember."

"Did you shake hands with Mrs. Cool?"

"I can't remember."

"Isn't it a fact that you did not shake hands?"

"I have no recollection in the matter."

"Why did you go to their office?" Quinn asked.

"Well . . . it's . . . it's——"

"Oh, Your Honour, I object!" Irvine said. "This matter has already gone far enough."

"The objection is overruled," Judge Lawton snapped.

"Why did you go to their office?"

"I wanted certain information."

"About what?"

"About rumours that were going around about a manufacturing establishment which was planning to locate in Citrus Grove."

"And didn't you mention at that time that you had real estate holdings in Citrus Grove?"

"I may have."

"And didn't you at that time offer to use your friendship

122

with the district attorney and your influence if Cool and Lam would co-operate with you?"

"Not in those words."

"But that was the idea back of your visit?"

"No, sir."

"What was the idea of your visit?"

"I wanted to get what information I could."

"And at that time and as a part of getting what information you could, you brought up the fact that you were friendly with the district attorney, and you did offer to co-operate in the case of the defendant John Dittmar Ansel, in case you in turn received co-operation from Cool and Lam?

"Yes or no?" Quinn thundered.

"Not exactly."

Quinn turned away with an expression of disgust. "That," he said, "is all."

Irvine announced the tests which were being made by the experts would require some time and suggested that Court adjourn until two o'clock.

Judge Lawton complied with the request.

"Meet me in your offices," I said to Quinn as he left the court-room. "I don't want to talk with you here."

I left the court-room.

Newspaper reporters were exploding flashbulbs in my face, also getting pictures of Bertha Cool.

One of the newspaper reporters asked Bertha Cool if she had any comments on Hale's testimony.

"You're damned right I have," Bertha said.

"What are those comments?" the newspaperman asked.

"You may say for me," Bertha said, "that Hale offered to use his good offices in getting the murder charge reduced to manslaughter if we'd give him certain information.

"You can also state that I'm willing to testify to that, and if that district attorney tries to cross-examine me, I'll tear his goddam can off."

I went to Quinn's office. Mrs. Endicott was with him.

"Well?" Quinn asked.

I said, "I want you to do one thing, Quinn. If you'll do exactly as I say we're going to come out all right."

"What is it?" Quinn asked.

I said, "Get the experts on the stand. Show that Endicott was killed with the Manning gun and not with the Ansel gun. Let everything else go by the boards. Concentrate on that."

I turned to Mrs. Endicott. "Did you bury that gun?"

She shook her head. "That testimony is absolutely unqualifiedly false."

"But," Quinn said, "how the devil am I going to prove it, Lam? If I put her on the witness stand, they're going to examine her concerning her movements on the night of the murder. Then they're going to smash her alibi."

"They're trying Ansel for the crime," I said.

"I know, but if they can discredit Mrs. Endicott it will reflect on Ansel. It will look as though the two of them planned the whole thing."

I said, "If you do what I tell you to, you won't need to put anybody on the stand."

"What?"

"Show the crime was committed with that gun that we turned over to the expert last night."

He seemed dubious.

"Damn it!" I said. "I know what I'm doing. Do what I tell you to and make the argument I tell you, and with that jury you're going to be all right."

"They'll convict him of something," he said.

"All right," I said, "it's an unfair question to ask you in front of your client, but what tactics do *you* have planned? Do you dare to put Mrs. Endicott on the stand?"

"No."

"Do you dare to put the defendant on the stand?"

"No."

"What's going to happen if you submit your case without putting either one of them on the stand?"

He made a grimace. "Ansel's going to be convicted of first-degree murder."

"All right," I told him. "You've got to do what I tell you to, whether you want to or not. Forget about your case. Concentrate on that gun, and when you make your argument, challenge the district attorney to tell the jury exactly what the prosecution claims took place. Dare him to reconstruct the crime for the jury."

Quinn was dubious. "He has the closing argument. He's smart. If I challenge him, he'll reconstruct that crime until the jurors will feel that they were in the room watching Ansel shoot Endicott in the back of the head."

"With the Helen Manning gun?" I said.

He thought that over.

CHAPTER TWENTY-THREE

COURT reconvened in the afternoon. The prosecutor recalled Steven Beardsley to the stand.

Beardsley testified that the expert employed by the defence and he had examined the weapon in question, that they had both come to the conclusion the weapon he referrred to as the second weapon was in all probability the one with which the murder had been committed. Beardsley testified also, however, that, while our expert had removed some samples of soil from that second weapon, enough soil remained embedded so that it was possible to obtain a soil classification.

This soil was entirely different in character from the soil found at the hedge and the soil which adhered to the gun which had first been introduced in evidence, the gun which he referred to as the Ansel gun. The second gun he referred to as the Manning gun.

There could, therefore, be no question but that the Manning gun had been buried for some period of time at a place other than in the hedge, that it had then been dug up relatively recently and placed in the hedge, that he could not of course state *who* had done this, but it had been done by someone.

The witness looked at Mrs. Endicott. She met his gaze with steady eyes and an expressionless poker face.

"You are satisfied that this weapon which you now refer to as the Manning weapon was the weapon from which the fatal bullet was fired?"

"Yes, sir. That is my opinion."

At the risk of being rebuked by the Court, I scribbled a note and had the bailiff deliver it to Barney Quinn.

The note said simply, "No cross-examination and rest your case at once!"

Quinn read the note, turned around and looked at me, frowned, thought for a moment, glanced at Irvine.

Irvine bowed sardonically. "Your witness, Counsellor," he said.

"No questions," Quinn said.

"That's our case. The prosecution rests," Irvine said.

"The defence rests," Quinn snapped.

Irvine was taken manifestly by surprise. "Your Honour," he said, "I ... I am completely taken by surprise at this turn of events."

"There's no reason why you should be," Judge Lawton said. "I feel that a veteran prosecutor should have been able to have anticipated such a move. Do you wish to proceed with your argument?"

"Very well, Your Honour," Irvine said.

Irvine made a great opening argument.

Quinn followed and talked about the peculiar circumstances in the case, the fact that the murder weapon had been brought home to the witness Manning, that while there had been an attempt by innuendo to show that Mrs. Endicott had buried something in the hedge, the prosecution had not shown what that was.

It was, Quinn pointed out, incumbent on the prosecution to prove its case beyond a reasonable doubt. It couldn't prove that Mrs. Endicott had buried *something*, and that at a spot near by other people had dug *something* up. It was incumbent on the prosecution to dig up every bit of earth in that hedge and show beyond all reasonable doubt that there was no other article buried there.

Moreover, he asked how could Mrs. Endicott have had possession of the murder weapon? *She* had not been in the house. If Ansel had wanted to kill Endicott, he would have killed him with the Ansel gun, not with the Manning gun. He certainly wouldn't have thrown his own gun out of the window in order to walk into the bedroom on the chance of finding a gun in the bedroom.

Quinn challenged the district attorney to reconstruct the crime. He said that he dared Irvine to show exactly how that crime had been committed.

Irvine grabbed a pencil and made notes. He was grinning.

Quinn sat down.

Irvine got up slowly, in a dignified manner. He announced that he would accept the challenge the defence had made in such a foolhardy manner. He said he would show exactly what happened.

He sketched Ansel, emotionally upset, blowing hot and cold. First he intended to kill Endicott; then he intended not to. He had thrown his gun away and had intended to leave the house. Then opportunity had presented itself and he had snatched the gun from the bureau and had killed Endicott.

Irvine stood up close to the jury box. His expressive eyes gazed into those of the women on the jury. He pulled out all the stops.

Judge Lawton instructed the jury that they had several forms of verdict: that they could find the defendant not guilty, that they could find the defendant guilty of first-degree murder, that they could find him guilty of second-degree murder, or they could find him guilty of manslaughter.

Judge Lawton defined murder in the first degree as being that which is perpetrated by means of poison or lying in wait, torture, or by any other kind of wilful, deliberate and pre-meditated killing, or which is committed in the perpetration or attempt to perpetrate arson, rape, robbery, burglary, mayhem or any act punishable under Section 288 of the Penal Code.

He instructed the jury that all other kinds of murders were murders in the second degree.

He instructed the jury that manslaughter was the unlawful killing of a human being without malice, that it was voluntary —upon a sudden quarrel or heat of passion.

He instructed the jury to select a foreman immediately upon retiring and to deliberate upon a verdict, and to have the fore-man advise the Court when a verdict had been reached.

The jury retired at four-fifteen.

Quinn came over to consult me.

"I don't get your strategy, Lam," he said.

"The court reporter took down the district attorney's closing argument," I said. "The district attorney walked into the trap. He claimed that regardless of what intent Ansel had had when he *went* to the house, he threw the weapon which he had with him out of the window. That constituted a renunciation of any attempt to commit premeditated murder.

"If the killing was committed with the gun lying on the dresser, the Manning gun, it had to be manslaughter."

"Well, that's exactly the way I feel about it," Quinn said, "and I'm afraid, terribly afraid, Lam, despite your optimism, that's the way the jury is going to feel."

"So what?" I said. "If the jury convicts him of first-degree murder, you can go to the appellate court and get the conviction reduced to manslaughter."

"And suppose the jury convicts him of manslaughter?"

"Then," I said, "wait until the Court discharges the jury and then come to the rail for a whispered consultation with me."

"I sure as hell hope you know what you're doing," he said. "I'd like to have gone after Hale. There's no question in my mind but what Hale went up the stairs after the defendant left, saw Endicott there in the bedroom, saw the gun on the dresser, shot Endicott in the back of the head, took the large sum of money that Endicott had with him, and which Endicott had apparently intended to use in paying off the twenty-thousand-dollar bonus he'd promised Ansel."

"Sure," I said, "we know what happened, but how the hell are we going to prove it?"

"Hale killed Endicott. He'd probably learned about the double cross Endicott had given his wife. He blackmailed Endi-cott for that. Then Helen Manning spilled the beans. Endicott would pay Hale no more blackmail.

"Hale tiptoed upstairs to listen. After Helen Manning left,

after Ansel left, Hale stepped into the room, picked up the Manning gun, killed Endicott and took the twenty grand.

"Hale buried the gun some place. After he learned Ansel had admitted throwing his weapon out of the window, Hale dug up the murder weapon he'd used and planted it in the hedge where it would be found. Then he said Mrs. Endicott buried it.

"We can't prove it, and we don't dare to try. Hale is a reputable banker now. He's used the capital he acquired to put himself across. He's a big toad in a small puddle. The district attorney has thrown the mantle of respectability over Hale's shoulders. He's the key witness for the prosecution. If you tried to prove he was the murderer, the jury would bring in a verdict of first-degree murder against Ansel. Then you couldn't do a damn thing about it. By fighting the case along this line, the worst they can give Ansel is manslaughter."

"They can put him in state's prison for ten years for manslaughter," Quinn said gloomily.

"Maybe," I said.

CHAPTER TWENTY-FOUR

It was eight-seventeen when the jury announced it had a verdict.

The jury came filing into Court. Some of the women had obviously been weeping.

The foreman of the jury, a grim-visaged, weatherbeaten rancher, announced to the Court that a verdict had been reached.

The Court went through the usual formalities, and the verdict was ready. The jury found the defendant guilty of manslaughter.

The foreman of the jury cleared his throat. "May I be heard, Your Honour?"

"What is it?" the Judge asked.

"The jurors unanimously expressed sympathy with the defendant but they felt that, under the law, it was necessary to convict him of manslaughter."

"Very well," the Judge said. "The verdict of the jury is received, and the jurors are discharged. Do counsel wish to set a date for sentencing at this time?"

Quinn said, "Just a moment, Your Honour."

He came over to the rail to confer with me.

"You have your Penal Code there?" I asked.

"Yes."

I handed him a slip of paper. "All right, read this to the Court."

Quinn glanced at the slip of paper. His eyebrows shot up. He looked at the paper again.

"The Court is waiting, Mr. Quinn," Judge Lawton said.

Quinn walked slowly back to the counsel table.

"If the Court please," Quinn said, "I feel that it is only fair to state to the Court that in this matter I have had the benefit of advice from Mr. Donald Lam, who has had a legal education. I have just received a document from him which is so startling I feel I must have time to digest it. However, the gist of what I have received is this: that murder is a crime which never outlaws. In other words, a prosecution for murder can be maintained at any time."

"There is no question about that, and no need to call that a startling doctrine," Judge Lawton said.

"The crime of murder," Quinn went on with a bow to the Court, "includes the crime of first-degree murder, second-degree murder and manslaughter.

"Now, however, we come to a very peculiar situation in the law. The crime of manslaughter outlaws within a period of three years. In other words, there can be no prosecution or conviction for manslaughter after a period of three years has elapsed from the date of the crime. Apparently the authorities are uniform on this, and since the defendant has now been convicted of a manslaughter which was perpetrated more than three years ago, the Court has no alternative but to release him.

"It is, of course, well known that a verdict of manslaughter constitutes an acquittal of murder in the first and murder in the second degree."

Judge Lawton looked at the district attorney. He studied Quinn. He looked at me. His forehead was creased in a frown, but I thought there was the trace of a smile at the corners of his mouth.

"Let me see that memo which was just handed to you, Mr. Quinn," Judge Lawton asked.

Quinn brought it up to the bench.

Judge Lawton ran his hand over his head. He reached for his Codes. He started studying the Penal Code. He looked up some of the decisions.

"Does the district attorney wish to be heard on this?" he asked Irvine.

Irvine said, "The district attorney is totally unprepared to argue this matter at this time, Your Honour."

"Well," Judge Lawton said, "there doesn't seem to be any room for argument. I note on this memo that Mr. Lam refers to the famous case of the so-called Spider Man, who lived for years in the attic of his victim. The defendant in that case was represented by Earl Seeley Wakeman. The same situation developed in that case.

"Now that the Court's attention has been called to that case, the Court remembers what was done at that time. The legal doctrine raised by the defence seems to be sound.

"I may say that, under the circumstances, the judgement which the Court is about to render is in accordance with the sympathies of the Court and apparently with the sympathies of the jury. The Court is not entirely convinced that some of the testimony given in this case is entitled to be considered at its face value.

"In view of the fact that the defendant has now been acquitted of murder in the first degree, and acquitted of murder in the second degree, and it appearing that the time limit has long since passed during which he could be prosecuted for manslaughter, the verdict of conviction by the jury is set aside, and the defendant is discharged from custody."

What happened in the court-room was little short of pandemonium. Spectators cheered. Newspaper reporters climbed up on tables, chairs, anything they could get hold of to take pictures.

I had characterized Elizabeth Endicott as being poker faced. For once, her emotions came through. Starry-eyed, she rushed towards John Ansel, threw her arms around him and kissed him with tears streaming down her face.

And then before I knew it, she was kissing me, babbling her thanks between kisses.

Judge Lawton gave up all effort to maintain order. He smilingly left the court-room.

Mrs. Endicott kissed Bertha. Then she kissed Barney Quinn.

Bertha Cool moved over to my side.

"You brainy sonofabitch," she said.

POSTSCRIPT

So far as Bertha was concerned, the case ended two days after the verdict when the cheque for fifteen thousand dollars came from Mrs. Elizabeth Endicott.

For me the case didn't really end until some weeks later when I received an envelope in the mail.

There was no return address on the envelope. It had been addressed in a neat feminine hand. It smelled of perfume. In the envelope was a newspaper clipping: "BANKER HELD ON CHARGES OF KIDNAPPING AND RAPE."

The clipping related how Cooper Franklin Hale, prominent Citrus Grove banker and head of the Hale Investment Company, had been arrested on the complaint of a Miss Stella Karis.

Hale, it seemed, had been managing some investments for Miss Karis. There had been a difference of opinion between the pair. Miss Karis claimed Hale had been using her money and her credit to back his own investments.

Hale had driven to the apartment of his client and suggested a ride to "talk things over".

Two hours later a motorist had picked Miss Karis up. She was covered with dirt and bruises, her clothes were ripped and torn until she was nearly nude.

She said Hale had stopped the car at a lonely spot, attempted to patch up their financial difficulties in a romantic interlude. When she refused, he had gone berserk. He had dragged her from the car and into the brush at the side of the road. There he had assaulted her.

According to Miss Karis, she had finally managed to escape only after her resistance had been overcome by brutal force.

Hale swore it was a frame-up. He said he hadn't needed to use any force.

I followed the case with interest. The jury believed Stella Karis, who made a terrific impression in court.

At this writing, Hale is doing time in San Quentin on a sentence of life imprisonment without possibility of parole.

THE END

>>> If you've enjoyed this book and would like to discover more great vintage crime and thriller titles, as well as the most exciting crime and thriller authors writing today, visit: >>>

The Murder Room
Where Criminal Minds Meet

themurderroom.com

9 781471 909009